D1603416

# TABLE LEGS

## Paul Lyons

NEW AMSTERDAM
*New York*

Copyright © 1989 by Paul Lyons
All rights reserved

Published in the United States of America by
NEW AMSTERDAM BOOKS
171 Madison Avenue, New York, N.Y. 10016

**Library of Congress Cataloging in Publication Data**

Lyons, Paul, 1958–
Table legs / Paul Lyons.
ISBN 0-941533-42-5
I. Title.
PS3562.Y4492T34   1989
813'.54—dc19                                                89-25840
                                                                 CIP

Printed in the United States of America

For Tony, Jenny, Charles, Mari, Nick, with love

Special thanks to Robert and Mary

*. . . the upper station of Low Life, which he had found by long experience was the best State in the world. . . .*

—Father Crusoe to his son Robinson

# 1

# Afternoon Casts

"Whadda you wanna do, young blood?" Table Legs says, leaning against the house counter, picking his gold front teeth with a toothpick.

"Hey Legs," I say.

"Baby, let's make a game. You and Legs. Stop all that trembling. Come on out now."

"Try you some one pocket, nine-six, Legs," I say.

"Lord have mercy, nine-six, you's handicapped in your heart enough already. . . . Take my money," he says, tosses a clipped roll of cash onto table one.

My heart catches at Franklin's profile.

"Police, he wants to rob me. Wants to stick up the Great Table Legs in broad daylight. Baby, you's stupid but you ain't deaf or nothing, you's got your own hands and feet. Play head up, baby. Your own fool self. Stop staring like a fool and make a game."

"One pocket, nine-six, get the balls."

"Never."

I spread my hands.

"Whadda you wanna do?"

"Take nine-seven and the break."

"Take, my ass. Take a chance like your funky grandfather Chris Columbus took a chance. Columbus had heart out in that rowboat, baby. Why ain't you got heart, baby? Quit stealing. Take a chance head up. That man took a chance."

"Yeah, and he's dead," I say.

Legs hikes up his black leather pants, adjusts the pouch at his side, walks with a lift to table one, sniffing the air hard. Muscles stranded and just starting to soften, he's maybe forty but with the older look of those who start early on the streets.

"Columbus ain't dead neither," he says, resting his elbows on the table. "And it stinks like scary white ass round here anyways. Make a game."

And for a minute I want to say *Okay, get the rack, sucker, you overgrown rack boy, take that wood necklace over your head and rack the balls tight,* and then whip him on the table until he's picking at his roll like it's an itchy scab, strip it all off him one time if I've got to lose a hundred sessions first, thinking if he breaks me so what, maybe being broke's about the best thing that can happen sometimes.

But losing's one thing, donating another. Without a spot Legs is too tough. He's been around and played big pool on the road and doesn't need to lose to me ever, no matter what the spot. His game isn't as sharp as it once was but he still knows the fine moves and the angles, can do things with the cue ball I don't know about. My money's peanuts to him, but he beats me flat out for low stakes for the fun of it, and I can't really mind losing to him, though losing always stings. I have to like the solidity of his game, watch-

8

ing him while I talk tactics and moves with the old-timers between shots, digesting what I can but only half-listening to them, the player's privilege, always half an eye on the action.

No, if I play Legs head up he'll bust me and I'll be out of action, hard money for weeks, nothing but the change found around the house, pulling back dressers and hunting the bottom of the washing machine for a recess quarter-pitching stake, the low road back through small parlays, and if all else fails selling mint plate blocks.

I've been standing in the shadowy doorway by the house counter and now I walk back into the stairwell and stuff my tie and jacket into my book bag, take out my shirt ends, rough the shirt, check my cash. Seven singles, two tens. The houseman grins at me through a chink in the hallway wall as I smooth the bills, tens on the outside, pocket them.

"Chipmunk," he says. "What you doing?"

"I'm here."

"You's here cause you ain't all there."

"Roger, Roger the Dodger."

"Going fishing?"

"Yeah Roger."

"Catch the Judge, table seven," and he giggles until his whole body's shaking wildly.

"Roger Roger," I say. "Watch it happen."

"Hit me on the way out, Chipmunk."

"I will."

"Can't run from me, young blood," Legs calls, still resting on the table, his face all glinting. "Go back out on the stairs if you ain't got no heart. You got to walk up the stairs like a man, baby. You got to stop that hide and seek shit, come on out of that funky playground now. You ain't gonna hide from no Table Legs."

Not hide but select, Legs. Not feed on the world in general because the big fish eat the littler ones, like once on a fishing trip with Dad and Hank upstate I saw a mammoth trout take a ten-inch chub sideways in his mouth. Hank and I were sitting eating ham sandwiches, plunking a corroded can by the stream with small stones, looking out over that still pool. Dad had caught a chub and thrown it back roughly. The chub swiveled slantways near the surface. At first the trout loomed up like a submerged log, hardly alive, then he was sharp, his great gills moving while the smaller fish—pale green and rust-colored— crossed in front, one second finning lightly, the next belly-wedged in the trout's mouth, head twitching but quickly stilled, the trout gorging him in two swallows, gliding, and full of slow slick power throbbing off into the deep water. Gone without a ripple.

"Jesus," Dad said.

And I looked over and saw Hank's mouth open too, and then the two of us were scrambling up the scree for our rods, pebbles raining, and casting in the direction of the trout, our silver C. P. Swing lures almost colliding in mid-air.

"Cast again," Dad kept saying, putting his own rod down while we lathered that pool, taking one last cast after another until it was too dark to see.

"Could a trout like that bite your leg off?" I asked

10

Dad on the drive home, squeezed in the front between him and Hank.

Now I wade deeper into the pool hall, away from Legs, who's moved over to lean on the house counter next to Roger, shaking his head about something, still picking his teeth, his straightened black hair rising in a wave, and I look out over the long room, checking the customers, options, breathing the action, the rows of rectangled green receding to wide bay windows, half with games going. Even in the grey slanting daylight smoke swirls upward in triangular shafts over the tables, the balls clicking with hard, crisp smacks, the action rising something sharp in my blood.

Hats Gonzalez misses a cut shot on the eight, his face barely moving when Rebel mops the table after him, then straining into a smile as he pays, like he's appealing to God without looking up. Rebel stuffs the bills in the pocket below his belly, and when one drops to the ground as he pulls his hand out stoops after it.

The Judge is practicing over on table seven sur-rounded by a bunch of dollar-a-game hustlers who hold maybe eleven dollars between them, shooing them away like flies, looking over his table and setting up shots, moving with his shuffle in a three-piece suit, shoes black and shiny, plump and juiceful as he moves, like honeydew melon.

I get him all in—multiple chins, the odd walk—in

one look, then turn fast so he won't catch me drooling.

He has a little tremor in his hand when he lowers on the balls, knows it makes him guide the balls when he should stroke them, knows the connection between ball and mind isn't straight because the fingers of his bridge hand just won't quite stay still for him. Sometimes I want to Krazy-Glue his varicose hand to the table, keep his knotted skittery fingers still so he'll shoot without spraining half the necks in the place.

He was supposed to be a pretty fair player back before he had a stroke, though even then he was a customer, basically of the nervous riche, his heart on the money ball, da da dum, dum da, and freeze. And now he can't beat anyone, just loves the action and the moments when his game comes together in a run, gels in a sequence, combinations. He is so cool when he makes a neat shot, never looks around, but I feel what it means to him, his deep vibration of pleasure, and I root for him, really I do, because when he makes a few good shots he doesn't care how much he loses, because the idea that a good player will reach into his pocket is so much stronger than the reality that he will probably have to reach into his own four or five times. And what a sweet coincidence of interests this makes for.

My whole body tingles; my arms fight the strain to wave him over. But I walk toward Legs and the house counter saying to myself, easy kid, peaceful, be calm. Check out a rack of balls, take it to the far end of the room, get a good stick, relax and enjoy the afternoon. Judge will be over, so much better to be fished for, and he must cast around for a way to donate his fifty or his hundred, won't feel right if he doesn't, but doesn't want to give it to a creep, make a creep's day and have to listen to the chirping. He must lose politely to someone shifty and smooth, not a gentleman but with the gentleman moves, someone who stays outside his vision while he shoots, stepping in only to hand him the chalk, attacking on the table.

Judge, I'm here.

"The baby," Legs whispers at me.

I get a rack and carry it on my shoulder like a bus tray over by the window, empty it across a table in the corner, turn my back on the balls, hearing their muffled caroms off the rails, their clicks and collisions fresh until they roll into place. I do not seem to notice Judge but all the time I am concentrating on him all the force of my will, dragging at him. He must see every slow movement of my back when I bend over the table for the first time, developing a sequence, figuring the position. The cue, back and forth, steadying, the axis of each ball almost painted on it like a street arrow to the pocket. He must know that in playing me he is playing someone with affection for the game matching his own, the pool passion that's an itch along the veins he hasn't had enough of, can't scratch without gambling now, can't ever get enough of.

He will not, cannot be right until he has felt the action, pressure of the money ball, left his fifty.

"Sucker got to relieve hisself," as Table Legs says. "Can't walk around holding, sucker don't feel right, got to relieve his funky ass."

And what's more, Judge has got to leave it all by six, ten after six max, when the phone rings and he shuffles over and has his little argument, poor Judge, the wife's voice practically rattling the receiver the way he holds it off his ear, occasionally raising his voice in token self-righteous opposition and then shuffling back in ribbons and saying, "Got to be the last game today, rack the balls, rack the balls, kid, hurry up."

Oh the neatness, the major chord of it all, like a Jaguar pulling up right on time for the getaway. To have played, profited, the bills spread later in piles of ones, fives, tens on the bathroom tiles, made good shots—and Judge must have good shots—and all in time to run home and make dinner, happy and sweaty, bounding into the kitchen to wash clean my chalk-crescented bridge hand over Mom's yell, "Not in the kitchen sink," wash until they are clean and then yell "What?" and hear her "Don't wash in the sink, Andy" and then, drying my hands, turn off the water with a "What?"

I stand by the window looking out over Broadway, school kids swirling up out of the subways, bright clusters bursting in different directions, running for busses or crossing the street arm in arm, and then I turn and walk to the rack and get a twenty-one-ounce stick, check the tip, rub powder between my bridge fingers. There's always a sweetness in holding back on the first shot, finding the key ball to get the sequence started, tasting the ripeness of the table, lie of the balls. And such sound business, because he's watching me, itching to ask for a game, exploring alternatives,

14

finding that there are none, just me practicing alone in the corner.

Oh why waste time, Judge. I know, you know, time's precious.

His eyes run all over me like hands; he's impatient with the creeps around his table trying to nickel and dime him into insanity with their clumsy greed, the degrading handicaps offered by those who, not holding, can bet any game. They nudge him, elbow him in my direction to where the balls spread lovely over the green felt with their arched slivers of shadow, their plumped sphericity, and I'm all busting inside to be freestroking, feeling that first rush of pool juice when the shots really come together, get compact, the control almost too fine, like I can't be touched, like the balls have eyes.

*They do have eyes.*

*And pockets are hungry mouths.*

"Hello, Judge," I say, looking up as if surprised, glad to see him when his drag shuffle stops at my table. There are veins along his eyelids, a twitch in his face that makes him blink as if in amazement; his cheeks hang watery below the jaw line.

"How are you feeling, Judge?"

"Okay, kid."

"How is everything?"

"Fine, kid, save the crap, rack the balls, rack the balls, kid."

"But Judge," I say, moving slow as I can, like I'm sleep walking, lining a cross-corner bank, false stroking deliberately over the ball, back and forth. "I'm not loose yet, Judge. Gotta get loose."

15

"The hell you're not loose. Rack em, kid."

"Shooting like Ray Charles, Judge. Can't see the balls, can't make a ball, stroke all crooked."

"Cut the crap, kid, or I'll walk. You don't want to play just say so."

His raised voice so gruff, but just a little smirk at it all inside somewhere, at one more crowning ridiculous fact. The cross-bank goes smack in like a barb.

Ah, but I'll play. And you don't know how sweet to me is that impatient music of the fake near-walk-away-cut-the-crap move, part of your pleasure, a little afternoon dirty talk, part of your act, your melody.

But now, Judge, seriously now.

You know better, Judge. We are not children. This is not an Egyptian flea-market. You must not bargain with me, become an embarrassment. This is Seventy-ninth Street and Broadway, the Guys and Dolls pool room. You will not walk and we both know it, not today, not until I let you—where would you go?—so you cut the crap and I'll cut the crap because we have an appointment. It is three-thirty; you are mine until six.

Then we can go to our families.

## 2

# Buddha, or the Pursuit of Greatness

*B*uddha gets me mucking about in these files, looming before me in his indigo shirt with upside-down parrots. His body slumps and is solid; the lenses of his glasses are thick. When I imagine the way he moves, his concentration, intensity, stillness, everything returns, the walks home in grey morning light, not a long walk but long when I'd lost, Table Legs and Scorpio.

Recently I've seen some of the old crowd, knowing by looking at any of them that none would have improved with time but that all would be more obsessive or sloppily drunk or in jail. Standing on the corner of Eightieth and Broadway Killer mumbles to me about how he's just lost in the crap game in front of the OTB, been up a bunch but not been able to quit, *eh eh eh, seven bring 'leven, 'leven bring seven, snake eyes you lose, shoulda quit, Andy, shoulda quit,* and I tell him I know, know how hard it is to quit sometimes, and when he asks me if he can hold five bucks until next week I tell him I'll give him three and we walk to an oriental grocery for change, and while I'm inside I buy a melon for myself and one for him, his eyes bulging when he takes it, looking at it like it's a giant amphetamine, like he's never seen a melon and might jump shoot it into a phantom wastebasket.

Now Guys and Dolls pool room is an Iranian rug shop with a new brown awning and a sign in windows covered from inside by rugs. I missed the boarding up, the layered graffiti, small colonies of *great* people huddled over the hot air grates near the awning.

Hilary and I went up there last week when I got a sudden interest in rugs. Up those stairs, twenty steps, rest, another twenty, steps I could still take blind, our padding feet strangely silent on carpet, the stairwell amazingly clean.

"Would you like to see any particular rug, sir?" a small dark man asked.

"No, no. I'm with her," I said.

Buddha sits cross-legged watching speed chess in the underground Game Room where I go once or twice a week after work to unwind; his eyes are deepset behind the wide-rimmed glasses. I can't quite place him. Two bearded old men are sleeping with their mouths open in front of an endgame. Myers the high school champ is playing Ginger the Bulgarian Master one-minute blitz. Ginger bets on anything— eating most, staying up longest, pissing farthest. During a backgammon tournament he played eight days without sleeping, ordering all his food. The slapping of the clock is fast, sporadic like border gunfire. I loosen my tie and watch off and on, trying to follow the hard crisp lines, get how they make the pieces co-operate, dodge the quicksand and roach motels, but they're beyond me. I couldn't follow them on a leash.

"Play some speed chess?" a Texan asks to Buddha. He's got a drawl and a belly that droops independent of the rest of his body, unhindered by a brass-buckled belt that pinches like the rope around a salami end, and he wears a shoe-lace tie held by a gold clip that glitters.

"No chess for money," Buddha says.

"Backgammon?"

"No, my game's pool."

And I place him.

"You do shoot pool," I say.

"Alrighty then," the Texan says. "If pool's your god-darned game. . . ."

"You don't want to do that," Buddha says.

"Don't be too sure," the Texan says, and calls to a man with a black leather jacket and sandy white hair, "Coop, this guy wants to shoot pool, there a place we can go to around here?"

"My car's outside," Buddha says.

"What are we waiting on, then?"

Buddha leans to me. "I'm only holding a bill," he says. "You want in?"

At first I'm amazed and thrilled he remembers me. It doesn't figure: I can't think I've seen him more than twice, and then he was playing, and that was eight-nine years ago.

"You in stroke?" I ask.

"In deathly stroke."

"All right," I say. "Better than sitting around."

19

"Anything's better than sitting around," Buddha says.

Memories of the last time I saw him shoot start coming clear. He destroyed Scorpio at nine-ball, making clean sequences of shots. I remember it all, Sweat Drops calling him Buddha because he was so at peace with his game, no one speaking to him, and not just because we felt bad for Scorpio, who had no business shooting him nine-ball, but would tangle with anyone.

"He just too good for me," Scorpio said, stripping the last tens off his roll.

So me, Buddha, the big Texan and Coop get into Buddha's old Dodge and head for Fourteenth Street, my briefcase squeezed between my legs in the front seat. Two styrofoam dice hang from Buddha's dashboard and a long green plastic skeleton.

Like most good pool rooms McGirr's is one flight up and has huge bay windows overlooking streets that are grey and noisy. I remember how in the late afternoons the light would slant through those windows in great shafts like cathedral light so I'd half expect organ music.

But now it's dark and the large panes reflect Texas going to the wall racks and choosing a heavy stick, rolling it over the table. While he's sanding it I take the ten through the fifteen balls off the rack, putting them in the slots above the ball return, and empty the one through the nine over the table and sit down next to Coop.

Now Guys and Dolls is a rug shop.

Hard to believe I haven't touched a pool ball in four or five years, haven't felt the old relaxing into an afternoon, sat with a black cherry soda looking out the window and then back at the table, someone concentrating there, but not me, from table level the balls gliding sleepily toward the rails and then darting off sleek and angular as spooked trout.

The last time I saw a table was six months ago at the party where I met Hilary. She was wearing a low-backed turquoise velvet dress and drinking from a martini glass. We gravitated toward each other. I thought I saw her lips gulp in her cigarette and then the cigarette reappear lit in her mouth. Incredible. When she spoke I sensed she was half-laughing at me but letting me hope she was at least a little charmed by my social awkwardness and that she too wanted to bag the etiquette stuff and find a quiet closet. I whispered in her ear.

"Ears are wonderful things."

At the bar I ordered orange juice on the rocks to ease me off a series of Walker Blacks and clear my head and Hilary ordered a Vodka Martini, dry.

"How's your juice?" she asked.

"It's pure, the real thing, the appellation's controlled," I said. "Want to try some?"

"Actually, I'm cutting back."

And a smile spread over her face, warming right through me, something binding beyond the kinetic, hormonal, anticipatory waves of the Glandular Imperative.

"What's the longest you ever went out with someone?" she asked after we'd talked about an hour.

21

"Where'd that come from?"

"Don't answer if you don't want to," Hilary said.

"I should answer. Four months."

"Really, a master of the short fling?"

"Just shy," I said.

"And waiting for the ideal woman?"

"No, no. My ideal woman wouldn't like me."

"But you'll settle?"

"Without becoming too settled," I said.

And there was the pool table, lovely and green, four by eight, almost glowing phosphorescent. A couple of guys from her firm were playing and smoking cigars and drinking cognac from large globed snifters and I looked at the smoke in the lights and felt heartsick. When they invited me to join I refused a bit too politely.

"Oh go on," Hilary said. "You look like you'd know how."

"Unpack that," I said.

"You've hardly taken your eyes off that table."

"And I thought they'd been mostly on you."

But I couldn't help watching, playing out the tight lines of attack, what to do on each shot, where to be safe or jugular immediately clear, tingling like instinct. It was late and their game had gotten quiet, gentleman serious. They had those glassy looks of concentration and mistaken sureness suckers always have. Smugness out of depth. I thought of bilking them slowly.

Texas slaps a few balls into the pockets and tests the roll to the corner. Buddha has brought his cue from the car and is screwing it together. It has simple, long diamonds of orange and green engravings up by the joint, a Palmer.

"I'm about ready when you are," Texas says. "What are we rolling for?"

"Two hundred a session?" Buddha says, not looking at me. "Race to five?"

"Sounds about right."

Buddha and Texas stand across the table and flip for break with a Kennedy half-dollar. Texas puts the coin back in his pocket and breaks and runs out to a duck combination on the five and nine.

"That's one," he says. "Mark up."

I move one bead over on the drooping string behind the table. Then I rack the balls, roll them square, press with the knuckles, lift.

"Thank you son," Texas says. "Now take care behind when I break."

The balls race around the table, ricocheting off each other, some disappearing into the pockets with a smack, the rest stopping across the table into an odd still-life, Texas hardly waiting until they're fixed before he rifles the one and through to the eight, moving fast between shots, pocketing cleanly, though his cue ball doesn't much feel the table under it. He hits the balls like he's angry with them, like they're dogs who've shit on the rug, his cue ball reckless. I remember the way Cigar Bill always polished the balls with Scott towels until they shone before practicing, how he set them rolling on the table one at a time. I remember cigar against Scorpio, the way I watched every move. Buddha stands out of the light, his face

23

wide and impassive in the shadows. One hand holds the cue at his side. He seems hardly alive, hardly breathing, his eyes great mica disks behind the flat lenses. He's not watching Texas's cue ball when it inevitably gets away on the nine and rolls and rolls until the cushion lunges out and freezes it fast.

"Sum bitch." Texas's voice is a whisper. "Too much green."

He stands back off the ball for a minute shaking his head and then reaches his cue out with one hand and taps the ball a half-inch off the rail, not enough, leaving too much shot, the nine white and yellow in the dead center of the table.

"I pushed out," he says to Buddha. "You want me to shoot?"

"No," Buddha says. "I'll shoot."

He walks slowly over to the powder rack and rubs a little white dust along the edge of his bridge fingers. He hasn't shot a ball yet, even to practice. He chalks around the cue-tip of his stick and lays the chalk gently on the rail of the table. Then he stands by the nine-ball for what must be a minute.

I'm fascinated. I can't imagine what he's thinking. I know that even when I was in everyday stroke I wouldn't have shot at that ball.

Buddha walks around to the end of the table and lines the ball. Back and forth goes his cue in measured half-strokes. Then he steadies and strokes the ball so cleanly and gently through the center of the pocket that it drops without a sound.

A bit of air escapes from Coop's lips.

"That's one hell of a player shot," he says.

I stare at the absence of the ball, feeling sick, dizzy. Then I realize I'm supposed to get up and rack the balls. My scalp tingles as I arrange them in the rack and roll and lift.

Buddha breaks the balls and runs the table.

When he breaks, the balls spread evenly on the green and one or two drop softly into the pockets and the cue ball freezes on command in the center of the table.

He breaks and runs out again, circling around balls, his cue ball dancing.

There's a flash of excitement when Texas takes out his roll and strips off two bills and puts back the gold clip and I know half of what it holds is mine, but after a few racks I don't care.

Buddha is thinking through sets of racks.

He breaks and the cue ball hovers in front of the one and he runs the rack. If he doesn't have a shot he pushes out long and follows with an immaculate safe. Every five games we get paid. Buddha doesn't lose a game. Texas doesn't exist for him anymore; I don't exist; no one exists.

For him there's just the position of the balls and the problem to be solved. Buddha just keeps nailing Texas to the table. Texas stands by the table riveted, his face strained in a hideous half-grin like a tanned Halloween mask, while Buddha's cue ball shifts and twists on the table as if his mind has it on leash, the draw so fine, the balls inching their way around, the cue like a nerved extension of his arm, cue ball never hitting a rail.

How has the pool room gotten away? It was going

already when, looking like a potential customer, I came back from college Junior year hoping to see the old gang and found instead the rug shop. I stood on the carpeted landing, remembering how my sneakers had always made a wet ripping sound with each bound up stairs sticky with spilled liquor and urine. Twenty steps, then the level, a long stride, then twenty steps, and I'd be at the top, hearing the irregular pool music of balls clicking, my blood moving fast. I stood on the landing to the rug shop but could not go up.

Buddha's carved out a system and lives in it. He's in a trance, intensely alive to his game, dead to all else, and I'm tingling all over as if in a fog by a cliff, like I could jump blind and trust there was water, the old thrill. He keeps nailing Texas down, nothing breaking the terrible stillness, the awful purity of his moves, nobody saying anything. Texas stands so still I doubt him the power to move without Buddha's permission. Every five games Buddha lets him move just enough to dip into the pocket below his belly.

I don't know how long the game lasts. Nobody could quit Buddha. Quitting Buddha'd be like calling Michelangelo off the scaffold after half a ceiling. When the game ends it's because all games have to end when someone can't pay, and there's no relief in its being over.

Then Coop and Texas are gone and I'm slicing the money into piles.

"Here's yours," I say to Buddha. "Count if you like."

"No need," he says, tucks the roll in the pocket of

that shirt of white parrots hanging upside down against a field of indigo.

I stuff my half in my jacket pocket. Neither of us moves. I'm holding my briefcase in one hand.

"That's the best pool I've ever seen," I say.

Buddha turns his eyes on me, nothing at all in his gaze, nothing I can see in him. He unscrews his cue and snaps the felt case around it, still looking at me, the large flatness of his eyes magnified by the lenses of the glasses.

"Shall we go have something to eat?" I ask Buddha in the entrance facing the dark street. "Would you like to go have a lobster?"

But Buddha gives so little evidence of hearing me I doubt he'd blink if I cracked him over the head with a cue stick. I open the door for him and he freezes for a moment, looking older than Sammy the Gin Player ever did, older than any man I've ever seen, the cars honking and the street bustling behind him.

"All I want," he says, "is one session of nine-ball with God."

# 3

# In Which the Hessel Family Dines

*T*here's a sweet vagueness about the clump of
Judge's money in my pocket during dinner. When I
get to the bathroom I will straighten the bills, sort
them in piles, fix them with a paper clip. I will not go
to the bathroom until I have to piss, count the whole
roll.

Because of a sore back from craning too long over
her paste-ups Mom sits in a low reclining chair that
squeaks like a baby chimpanzee. Chest high to the
table, she has to reach in a way that makes her exem-
plary napkin and fork work comic and unavoidable.
We're all silent watching her work, mesmerized by
the slowness with which the knife draws across the
fork-held chicken, almost stroking it, and then, in
chop-stick-like tandem, knife and fork daub the slice
in a circle of gravy in the center of the plate and bring
the meat to rest on the dry raised edge. When she
looks up and catches us all watching she blinks fast
several times, sets her fork and knife down, waits for
someone else to move.

"Cranberry sauce," George says, and starts to snake his arm across the table for the dish.

"Will you pass the cranberry sauce, please?" Mom says, late intercepting his arm, then separating it from the sauce and passing the dish to him.

"Thank you, Mother dear," she says, when he forks a mound on his plate.

"Thanks Mom," George says, mouth half-full.

"Good day at school?" Dad asks me.

"Pretty good," I say.

"Play some ball?"

"Yeah," I say.

The sprint home from the pool room has soaked my shirt. I've started using the ten-block dash to test how hard my body can go. I pretend I'm being chased and floor it early, dodging traffic onto West End Avenue and then trying to shift into even higher gear, dust the phantom pursuer, banking into the turns; halfway home I'm out of air, stabbing pain through the shoulders, a lifted and woozy feeling, but I push harder against the outer envelope until my legs go lactic under me. On our block I stop, fold my hands on top of my head, and, gasping, let the sweat come in a slow walk to our brownstone steps.

"Hit a few?"

"Yeah, I was on."

"Full court?"

"Yeah."

"The guys there?"

"Some of them."

"How about you, George?"

And I look up and see George smiling faintly at me

with cranberry-reddened lips and know he's spent the whole afternoon at the courts and can fry my ass with an eyebrow movement. There's a flash of ninth-grade knowing in those small brown eyes, his hair too bushy long for the pinched active face, the bony frame that's constant motion, burning calories. Since he surprised me at the pool room he's known some-how what concealing it means to me, and known how to milk it, and his silence will be extortionary. His look says, *You owe me and boy do you owe me and you'll pay me or I'll leak all over you.*

"What you want?" Roger asked him. "Ya'll can't be coming in here now."

"Run his ass out of here," Table Legs yelled.

George stood staring from one of them to the other, his mouth open, and just pointed at me. I was in the middle of a run and missed when I saw him.

"It's okay, he's with me," I said.

"That's right," Table Legs said. "Cuss him out, run his funky white ass out of here, he's with the baby."

"That your kid brother?" Freddie the Fish asks.

"Yeah," I say.

"Hey kid brother," Freddie says to George, who still hasn't moved.

We walk over by the phone booth.

"Dad's real pissed you're late," George says, still looking at Roger and Legs and out over the tables and the smoky lights, his eyes hyperactive.

"Ya'll cutting a deal?" Roger yells. "Don't be doing that shit in here, Chipmunk."

"Chipmunk?" George says.

And I go over to the table where I'm shooting

31

Killer eight ball for fifty cents a game and the time. Killer's sitting on the table with his eyes bulging out and I say, "Bet off, I got the time."

George and I jog home side by side, first silent, then whistling in sync the martial tune we learned in Summer Camp. When we're on the stoop George says, "I said you were at the courts."

"Thanks, kid brother," I say.

And we whistle up the stairs into the dining room, stopping side by side, Sarah directing the tune with her hands in the air into a crescendo.

"Wash your hands," Mom says. "Both of you."

"Chicken's good, Mom," Hank says, voice full of taste. "There's ginger. What else? No, did you shred fresh coconut into this sauce?"

Oh what a maestro of civilities he's become, slick as his hair, the poet laureate of our dinner table, and looks which make me wonder sometimes if he's really my brother. He's always been there up ahead, instructing me in the fine points of dirty stamp trading or the behind-the-back dribble, but he's the only one with blue eyes; his hair's too straight and black for the rest of the family—now he wears it parted in the middle to display more forehead—and he's about eight inches taller than me. An endocrinologist predicted I'm due for a growth spurt soon and will achieve normal height, but at my age Hank was an inch shorter than he is now and had his own ivory-handled shaver and face brush on display in the bathroom. He'd walk the hallways half-lathered looking for towels. I bet the guys in my class I'd make five-ten and they just rolled their eyes. If I were a parent and had adopted a child, at what point, re-semblances permitting, would I let it be known?

"Can't we turn off that air-conditioner?" George asks, pointing at goose bumps on his arms.

"There is a slight danger of frostbite," Hank says, since he's right in the arctic stream of the thing.

Mom's imploring look to Dad suggests that the cool civilized air is the only thing between her and heat prostration.

I think of recommending salt tablets but control myself.

"Turn it down halfway, Henry," Dad says.

George excuses himself and walks downstairs and bounces back in wearing his winter jacket, Eskimo-furred hood drawn up and tied so his face is barely visible. When Dad sees the coat he takes a deep breath, pulls his chair in closer to the table with a quick hop. He looks exhausted, his tie hanging loosely around his neck, the top buttons open. His expression says he only wants and deserves a little peace with his family after a long day.

I look across and want to say something nice or at least something intelligent to him to make up for the lies I've told but think, *There's all kinds of lying, decep-tions that are more withholding truth than telling lies, generous deceptions, you made it to the dinner, relieved Old Judge of a little excess cash, who's the worse for it all?*

"Sarah, what did you learn in school today?" Mom asks, though I can feel the "you" and "learn" itching all over me and George like poison ivy, as if address-ing the question to hopelessly unserious people like us would be futile.

33

The question can't touch Hank, just done with Sophomore year at Columbia in this last week of April—college has that going for it—with yet another Dean's list swinging from his belt like a scalp; he squeezes his eyes shut for a few seconds, then looks affectionately at our little sister.

When George interrupts Sarah's answer she goes into her patented sulk, sinking in her chair until her eyes are table level.

"You're a stupid idiot," she whispers to George.

"Most idiots are stupid, mental midget," George says.

"Daddy," she says, trying to look hurt and angry, but the hint of smile showing she half-knows what's coming. Malice just isn't convincing on freckled people.

"Daddy, nobody lets me talk around here."

George and Hank and I look at each other, the temptation simply too strong and simultaneous, even for Hank, who joins in for old time's sake, "Awwww-wwwwww."

Hank smiles, then remembers where he is, dabs his mouth with a napkin.

"Poor wittle Sawah," George whispers from under his hood, just loud enough for her and me.

She slaps his jacket.

"It's true you don't let her get in a word edgewise," Mom says.

"Edgewise?" George asks, looking at me knowingly.

*Remember the courts?*

Okay, I return his little smile.

34

"Is this all necessary?" Dad says, slamming his hand on the table. "George, what are you doing? Take that damn coat off now."

"Ahhhhhhhhhh."

The sudden slam of the hand; a quick clatter of china, Grandma's silverware giving a little hop on the table.

And there are a few minutes of silent serious eating, Dad going so fast that it'd be best to keep fingers away from his plate, cubes of light from the crystal overhead dodging and bending over the dishes as George and I move simultaneously for a piece of chicken with particularly crisp breaded skin, slightly juice-soaked, both recoiling instinctively, paralyzed in a motion jinx, fork hands at our sides like gun-fighters, before he draws on the chicken and has it speared on his plate.

# 4

# Guys and Dolls

*T*he first time I played pool was with Dad at about fifteen. We started going every few weeks after Sunday B-ball and as we walked up Broadway, tired and sweaty from beating against taller players, I could taste the first black cherry soda and the lagging for break and then the slow game of straight pool to fifty, seventy-five if I could talk out an extension. Once we went to two hundred, score kept close and tense all the way. Dad must have played a lot in his college fraternity and in the Army, but not much since, and he knew enough to show me little moves before our sessions, demonstrate draw or follow, some rudiments of position. He would try to get me to spread the fingers of my bridge hand, but out of persistent assholery I stuck six months with the balled up vee formed by thumb and index fingers that I now recognize as one way suckers reveal themselves.

We stopped about a year ago, and I've quit suggesting a game. I slip off after ball and when I get back a few hours later Dad and Hank are still in sweats watching a ball game or fight.

"Holding the stick right yet?" Dad asks, though he really wishes I didn't shoot so much, or at all.

The last time we played I whipped him at half-speed and he must have felt the holding back and seen that the half-misses, control, implied cockiness of easy position came from hours of practice and gambling, not genius. I'd freestroke a few—too hard, too much English, but with an open touch—wanting to show what I had, how I'd grown; then, not wanting to show too much, I'd dog a ball so he could run some. Narrow misses into an open table. I guess he knew.

Sweat Drops came over and sat on the table next to ours, chattering to me out of the side of his mouth, shabby in a long ragged overcoat with layers of uncleanness, upset as usual with some gross unfairness in the world and incapable of looking a clean person in the face.

Dad was polite to him, listening and agreeing with a few of his beefs—that politicians were basically sick bastards, Sweats learned that in Nam, that you can't even get a decent burger anymore because everyone uses horsemeat. But later, walking home silent, I could feel the chafing of Dad's disappointment, disappointment that I'd played enough to know people in the pool room and had started picking up some of their moves and language, disappointment that if I was playing too much he was in some way to blame because he'd encouraged it and because at sixteen, too short to be believed any other way, he'd shown the houseman my birth certificate which meant I could go to the pool room whenever I wanted.

At first I played a half-hour once in a while before dinner, but then I started getting feverish at the ends of dinners and had to keep myself from bursting off my seat by an exertion of will; I started thinking about the game all through classes, diagramming runs in notebook margins, and spending long afternoons shooting against old Sal, who once played third base for a Chicago White Sox farm team, but never got called up.

Sal's face is a sea of wrinkles, his hands massive and firm. He wears his pants high and with suspenders and has a slight stoop in the shoulders. When there's no action we still play a Garcia Vega cigar against a black cherry soda for a session of one pocket, me sharpening my game against his experience, him half-accepting himself as pool guru teaching discipline, passing on control, mental calm, the conservative play that makes hotheads bust themselves, half-spiteful and pissed off at being old and beatable, hating the haughtiness and looseness in his opponents and his own pool knowledge that his loss of power is another's gain, but that he can't fold because of his knowledge.

His vision's inconsistent so he can't shoot the long shots anymore though he's still master of the positional safe. He'll safe a dozen times running even when he has straight shots. He chews on the butts of unlit cigars between shots and cusses to himself and when I turn the cue ball loose on fancy shots mumbles "asshole" at me and studies the table harder, looks up and says, "Don't improvise so much, think it through" and false-strokes and looks up again to say,

"Without position you're just a punk. Go have fun, amuse yourself," and studies harder for moves to stitch me with, working for an edge, moving the balls to his side.

There's a running crap game played against a cardboard box in the back and I ring against the walls with Freddie the Fish and Panama, shooting Table Legs or String Bean for a fin, String Bean enormous and bald, rubbing his soft black shoulders against the wall like a cat, cupping the dice in his hands and blowing on them, schooling them against the wall.

Bean should rent himself out as a grandfather.

I'd rent him but he wouldn't get along with Grandma, who fancies herself one of the greatest liberals of the twentieth century but insists all negroes are scared of heights. What anyway is wrong with being scared of heights? All Grandma and Bean'd have in common is the habit of swiping pocketfulls of ketchups and mustards from McDonald's, and Bean'd never get used to Connecticut where all the action's rigged—Cubans dropping jai alai balls, dogs getting fed meatballs so they won't chase the mechanical rabbit.

"Whadda you wanna do?" Legs says to me. "Let's make a game."

"We're shooting dice."

"Make a game, baby, you gotta relieve yourself."

"Try you some nine with the eight-wild."

"Not Legs."

"Call the eight and the break."

"Head up, baby. Quit that stealing shit. Quit it, baby. This is Legs, baby. This ain't no Santa Claus.

40

You see any reindeers around here, baby? This ain't the welfare man. Talk to Legs, baby."

"Got to give up something," I say. "Got to give me a chance."

"Ain't no one gonna *give* you nothing."

"Legs wouldn't give you ice water in winter," says Freddie the Fish. Freddie wears a tire pressure gauge in his front pocket—*Couldn't pass it up for a buck, kid*—and it sits in the scruffy flannel shirt like the pocket thermometer of a homeless doctor.

"Make a fair game and I'll play, Legs."

"Ain't no fair games, baby. Sucker like you ain't never 'sposed to win."

Legs's head moves fast when he talks, shaking off what you've said, nodding as he straightens it.

"You's too scary," he says. "Ain't got no heart at all. You's scared of your own face, can't say I blame you neither. Pity the mirror, baby."

"I'll race you around the block for a hundred, head up, Legs, take a chance.

"He couldn't walk around the block," Freddie says.

"Pushups, Legs."

"Fuck that exercise shit, baby. Won't never catch me lifting no finger. Shoot pool, baby, show you got heart. This ain't a gym, only a few white dumbells in here. Take a chance, baby. Funky Columbus took a chance."

Now every time I hear his name I picture Columbus rowing around the tourmaline Caribbean with nine emaciated Spaniards. I'm not sure why.

"Five open, who wants it?" String Bean says.

"Six the point."

41

"Five more on the Bean," Legs says.

"Faded Legs," I say, dropping five on his.

"Six him Bean," Legs says. "C. I. X. on his scary white ass. Lord Jesus six on his ass. If the Bean don't six there ain't no Jesus, make it eight-six."

"Faded eight-six."

"Eight skate and donate," Bean says. "Catch em dice. . . . Come to . . . Mama."

"School those dice," Freddie says when Bean hits. "Make em behave."

"School days," I say, shooting them a few times, then pushing them back to Bean. "School days."

And the dice against the cardboard, the afternoons sliding away, the cash changing hands, Legs yelling "Lord have mercy dice" after every roll, and when the dice go bad Freddie cursing, a right better who never lays on himself, convinced he *ain't got no luck* from years at the track, but who can't let another shoot in peace. A man of insane superstitions, Freddie won't let Hats Gonzalez walk behind him or a man change dice hands when rolling.

"You let him do that to you, kid?"

"Do what, Freddie?"

"Whadda you walk around with your hands on your ankles? Switch hands on you, kid. He's switching. First he rolls with his right hand and then with his left hand."

"He's ambidextrous, Freddie."

"He's ambi-dick-strous, kid. Don't let him switch on you. Make him roll like a gentleman."

# 5

# Scorpio

*S*corpio has a way of just appearing or disappearing. His hair's slicked back over his head and there's a smoothness and bounce to his moves, an extra swivel. He calls in takeout Chinese for Sammy the Gin Player and the old men who watch along the walls and he goes into the bathroom with hookers for cocaine. Nobody knows where he's from, guy like Scorpio seems to float, but he's in every few weeks, shooting a sweet stick like a top player on the road, risky but tight, best against players he's not supposed to beat, playing with all the gentleman moves, out in the shadows while his opponent lowers, but still a killer in the big game, fighting off the tiredness that comes in surges for as long as it takes. Never a grinder, never a wearer down, never precise, always after the aggressive shot that breaks open a position, like a fighter who keeps the steady pressure on and cuts the ring and knows how to finish with an accurate and terrible flurry.

He waits with a toothpick in his mouth near where Cigar Bill practices on the player table, his cue flicking between his bridge fingers like a snake's tongue, making a dozen lightning false strokes.

"Here to play, Scorpio?" Cigar says, not taking his eye off the ball he's been aiming at for maybe five minutes.

"Yeah, Ceegar."

"Good," Cigar says.

He's an old timer, treats the table like a rare manuscript, shines the balls on the thick plaid wool of his shirts. He likes to smoke fat cigars while he plays, set them on the rail and puff away, to stand over the table and study the lay of the balls. When he's going there's a rhythm to his moves, the way he chalks his stick, wipes the felt of the table with a paper towel; there's a lulling creaky quality to his pace, his steps. He'll stand by a ball chewing his cigar, half asleep with his eyes open in front of it.

Now he's false-stroking slower at the ball, cue moving steady through his bridge, back and forth, winding everyone's heads on their necks.

"You trying to make friends with the ball, Ceegar?" Scorpio says, stepping into the light.

But Bill just looks up at him like he's ignorant of higher things, like he's a piss-ant, snaps his suspenders and goes back to the ball, measuring out the diamonds on the edge of the table with his eyes. Then he moves for the powder rack, coats between his fingers, blows smoke from his cigar, stands back over the ball, still amazingly solid in the same place.

"Rack the balls, Scorpio," Bill says, and rolls the ball to the head of the table, everyone exhaling with a gasp when at last it moves, as if a bronze statue has suddenly mooned us.

They lag for break. Bill's lag practically kisses the rail, and when he breaks a few balls move toward his hole and the cue ball caroms two rails to the farthest corner. Scorpio smiles and walks round to the ball.

"Good break, Ceegar," he says, and plays a neat safe, kicking a ball free from behind.

I take a seat by the wall. The clock says I'm missing dinner.

Mousey the Thief comes in holding a huge chandelier and walking from player to player asking fifty bucks for it. His head's small, cheeks thin, jerking back and forth like a bird's; his eyeballs are the fattest part of his body.

"Thing's worth a grand, man, take a half C for it."

The crystals throw prom-ball light speckles all over the walls as he walks with it, constellations of colored light like that projector in the planetarium.

"Get away from me, you lobster," Sammy the German gin-player says.

Sammy's eighty-nine and always leaving quarters on the arm of his chair to see who'll swipe them.

"Those thieving bastards," he says, his voice faint and cracked, winking at me, turning away as Rebel shambles up and puts his hand on the quarter.

"Look, look, look, look," Sammy whispers to me. Then, "Rebel, what's under your hand?"

"Quarter."

"Take your fat hand off it."

45

"Why?"

"It's mine."

"Was yours."

"I left it there to check on you, you . . . you fathead."

"Yeah, really? Put another one there."

"Make him behave, Samula," Freddie says. "Discipline him."

"Whip his funky ass," Legs says, a pained smile creasing and lighting his face like crinkled black tinfoil. "Lord have mercy, whip his ass."

"No violence, Sammy," String Bean says. "Don't be a gorilla, Sammy. Give him a break."

"I'll break his fucking arm," Sammy says, beaming in his high seat, laughing into a cough that swells the veins on his head and makes him drool.

"Wipe your face, Sammy," Freddie says. "You're not at home. This is a gentleman's club."

Sometimes when Sammy's in a bad way and can't talk Freddie gets up a collection and brings the Szechuan menu and has Sammy point to what he wants and when the food comes he forks it into Sammy's mouth and wipes up his shirt and face where drool collects.

"Somebody take this thing off my hands, swear it's worth a grand, giving it away for half a C," Mousey says.

"Get away from me, you lobster," Sammy says, waving his stick hands at Mousey.

"Thing'd burn my hands off," Freddie mumbles. "Got smoke coming off it."

46

Everyone puts their hands on their cash as Mousey passes.

"Sucker'd steal the cuffs off a cop," Freddie says.

Standing next to Andre the Great, an immaculate Puerto Rican trick-shot practicer always dressed in a three-piece suit, wavy hair slicked back over his head all ridges, I watch every move that Scorpio and Bill make, savoring the positions of the game played at a level so much higher than my own. Andre nudges me after every shot, pursing his lips and making small nods that ask if I've seen what he's seen.

Bill moves slower and slower, as if his legs have to think out where they're going. He concentrates into the balls, brooding, lulling them, nothing but methodical. Safe, safe. Another game winds down, safe, safe. Someone pockets, slow rolls to the hole, more safes. Then there's one ball left and whoever makes it wins. Cigar banks it for the hole, controlling the speed and the length, coaxing the ball nearer and nearer to home sweet home. He banks two rails using wide-angle English, rolling the ball to his hole, Scorpio knocking it back and away, Bill getting it closer and closer until it lies in the hearth of the pocket and there's no way for Scorpio to escape, no way Houdini could escape in ten tries.

Scorpio swings behind Bill's pocket, steps catlike, chewing. He lowers over the cue, angular jaw working like he's chewing steel, like I've never seen a jaw working, almost like the jaw's thinking, cords of muscle and tendon shooting through cheeks growing greyer by the minute. His cue tip flicks in a few fast half-strokes and he steadies and then the cue ball starts approaching the ball, cautiously at first, feeling its way, slow motion to the object. It inches toward the ball and hesitates and then at the last moment does a thing a pool ball just doesn't do.

Throw physics out the window.

Somehow the object ball dodges the cue kiss and hits the point of the pocket and changes direction and heads for Scorpio's pocket. It starts slowly and begins to gather energy from within and move and the whole crowd that's watching starts to sway in place and just roll and lean with it and lean more until everyone's bent toward the ball and when the ball finally falls into the pocket with a little smack a collective gasp almost floats the table.

"Ave Maria, ave Maria," Andre the Great mumbles next to me, running his hands over and again over the slick ridges of his hair, moaning something to himself in Spanish. His eyes look about to jump out of his head. He wipes his forehead with his tie and then catches himself holding the tie and looks around to see if anyone's noticed and tucks it back under his vest.

"Scorpio, Scorpio, hey, hey," Sammy the Gin Player says.

The old men by the walls light up like slot machines.

"Damn good shot," Cigar says, whistles. "God damn."

He's happy, almost shaking as he pays out five tens, like a bank teller, giving each bill a little snap.

Andre keeps looking at the table and then at his hands and then back at the table, running his hands through his hair, whispering, "Ave Maria, ave Maria."

The move is miraculous. Scorpio comes over and leans against the wall next to me. Two guys have fished the nine-ball out of the pocket and are trying to understand how it could be cross-banked off the inside lip of the pocket without scratching. They are arguing and shaking their heads.

"Through for the night," Cigar says, unscrewing his cue.

"That was a hellified shot. A hellified shot. House, I'm off. Take it down. Back in the morning."

Andre comes over and shakes Scorpio's hand.

"Someday I show you that shot, kydd," Scorpio says to me.

# 6

# School Days

*D*uring lulls at school I see this black three card monte player reeling around behind a cardboard box mounted on a garbage can, a bottle of Cold Duck jutting from his threadbare pocket, his eyes rolling, his whole body swaying like he can't possibly keep himself upright much longer, in one hand an insanely large roll of cash, tens, twenties, I mean at least a grand, calling, *Get on it, who see it, get down, who see the red, who see it,* putting the cash in his pocket, *Who see the red?* And then holding the cards up slowly. One at a time. *The black, the black, the red, the black, the black, red. There she is. Who see it? Damn,* he says. *No-bod-ee see it,* and he holds the red straight out for everyone to see, holds it out at our faces like he's challenging us to rob him and then sets it flat down on the cardboard, pulling out the cash again and waving it, the whole thing ridiculously plain, like stealing pencils from blind men. *Now who see it?*

And when no one moves he turns it over, the red just where we all knew it was.

*There it is. The red.*

A Hassid all in black and white who's been watching, freezes, begins to shake all through his body, vibrates in place. He's so excited he can't speak and when he does his voice shakes, saying, *Again, again, do it again,* a hunger in his eyes, theft in his face, do it again. And the black guy does it exactly the same; we all see it, the black guy drunk, high, insane, about to chuck his grand to the wind. He holds the red card in front of our faces and then sets it down. *Who see it? Who see the red?* And the Hassid clears us away from the board, *Nobody touch it, nobody move, I see it, I see it,* thinking he's got the monte player now after all his losses, for once has his balls in a vice, is as sure of it as he's ever been sure of anything. *I see it.*

*For how much?*

*For three hundred if you got guts.*

*I got guts,* the black man says, still staggering in place, back grazing the parked cars, everyone on the side wanting to say to him no, no, no, no, don't do it you drunk fool, we all see it, or to get down themselves, bet their payroll, lay down the mortgage, family jewels, the Christmas money, the thing's so plain.

*Get down on it,* the black guy says, fumbling until he's counted out three hundred. *That all you want? There's more. Who wants some? Get it up.*

The Hassid opens his wallet, draws out three crisp bills that look straight from a Chinese laundry, his hand trembling as he sets them by the monte player's.

*Choose.*

The Hassid reaches for where we know it is.

*Choose that red.*

He grabs it, clutches the card, then turns it where everyone can see.

*Black.*

Stands with it stunned.

*Black.*

Turns up the others frantically.

*Black.*

*The red.*

When the school bell rings the door clicks shut behind Gavin, who moves to his desk, snaps open his briefcase, takes out a stick of chalk and then shuts the briefcase, his presence snuffing the buzz of conversations so quickly that an involuntary titter follows the silence. Gavin erases the blackboard, already blank, evening the chalk smudges, and writes so hard on the board I wonder why the chalk doesn't break. He's tall and incredibly thin with hair that rises real and ungreased in an immovable serried wave, a notched scalene triangle.

GETTYSBURG    SHILOH    COLD HARBOR APPOMATOX

Gavin swings in front of the desk, rests his hand on the bumps of his hair, quiet of the room amplifying the overhead hum of lights as he looks us over, taking mental attendance, his head bobbing at each momentary eye contact.

"Yes," he says, backing around to the board and underlining "Cold Harbor" twice.

"Cold Harbor," he says, softly. Then a few decibels

higher, sharp enough to fix everyone's posture in their seats. "Cold Harbor."

"Miss Kendrick, why did I underline Cold Harbor?"

"It was a major battle."

"In what campaign, Miss Kendrick?"

"The Overland Campaign of 1864."

"Good. Good. Very good. Describe that campaign for us a little, would you, Mr. Levy."

Levy's stumped and slumps in his seat, looks around uncomfortably for a supportive grin, starts reddening. He's a harmless idiot, gets subterranean grades. In the lunch room Jonesy and Al have a way of counting to ten so that he'll laugh so suddenly while drinking milk that the milk streams out of his nostrils and soaks his face. Then they act like they're pulling spaghetti out of their noses to imitate the milk streams and he practically chokes. Now Gavin takes the aisle in four strides until he's enormous over Levy's desk.

"Mr. Levy, do you read me?"

Several hacking coughs.

"Mr. Levy, what language do you speak at home? Shall I call a translator?"

Levy shakes his head, starts to speak but stops, knowing if he tries to say anything he'll only dig his grave deeper.

"Mr. Levy, what do you intend to do when you leave this institution? Maybe you would like to be an auto mechanic. Would you like to be an auto mechanic, Mr. Levy?"

"What's wrong with being an auto mechanic, sir?" Levy blurts out, and half our heads hit the desks.

"Ah," Gavin says after a silence, "ah, Mr. Levy," turning his back on Levy and walking to the front, nodding. "Nothing at all, Mr. Levy. Nothing at all. Carry on. Don't let us disturb you."

When he turns, his face is screwed into a scowl. Silence builds; outside a dog yelps fanatically as if it's had its paw smacked with a ruler. Gavin nods in the directions of the sound like the dog's another insolent student.

"Frankly, I'd have that dog stuffed for the Museum of Natural History, canine wing," he says. "At Cold Harbor many of the soldiers pinned their names to the backs of their blouses. Why would they do such a thing, Miss Phillips?"

"Maybe because they didn't expect to live and they wanted their bodies to be taken care of."

"Taken care of," I hear, and "taken . . . care . . . of" echoes through this vision of Gavin nostril-tubed in one of those hospital spaces defined by plastic curtains like a shower, the kind that makes you think if you ripped them aside suddenly you'd find naked persons soaping each other.

*Mr. Gavin, are you in pain? Where does it hurt, Mr. Gavin? Don't worry, Mr. Gavin. You will be taken care of.*

"Taken care of. Good. Very good. Mr. Hessel?"

*Can you put your hand to where it hurts, Mr. Gavin? Mr. Gavin, did you once throw Andy Hessel's notebook out the window? Did you shred a paper of his in front of the class? Was that a pedagogically sound thing to do, Mr. Gavin? Mr. Gavin, we're going to give you a shot now.*

And a grim nurse with a pencilled moustache makes for him, pointing an immense hypodermic with his left ass cheek written all over it.

"Mr. Hessel, just how many soldiers were there in the Union assault?"

"Forty thousand soldiers."

"Good. And do you remember, Mr. Hessel, how many of those soldiers died that day?"

"About ten thousand?"

"Seven thousand, Mr. Hessel, and a thousand on the Confederate side. Why such disproportionate casualty rates, Mr. Hessel?"

"Because the Union attacked up a hill. The Confederates waited and then opened up on them."

"Good. Who led the attack?"

"General Grant did."

"Good. Who defended?"

"Lee."

"General Lee. Yes. Do you remember what the Confederate army opened up with, Mr. Hessel?"

"Cannons and rifles, wasn't it?"

"Yes, and what was in the cannon, Mr. Hessel?"

"Wouldn't it be cannon balls, Mr. Gavin?"

That gets a few groans, fists pounding desks.

"No it wouldn't be, Mr. Hessel. Cannon balls were used for levelling structures or destroying enemy cannon. The Confederates waited on the hill at Cold Harbor with modified cannon loaded with grapeshot and bits of iron and scrap metals, scrap metals, Mr. Hessel, no joking matter. . . . Mr. Bender."

56

Lord have mercy, he's off me.

"Mr. Bender. Some historians say Cold Harbor was a success for the Union. Seven thousand dead in one day, piled on each other, the Rebel Army themselves horrified at the butchery. How might this be considered a success?"

"I don't see how, Mr. Gavin."

"Think, Mr. Bender. I know the activity doesn't come naturally to you, but you do think, don't you? Your mind's not Swiss cheese. Nod your head to indicate the affirmative. Was that an affirmative or not, Mr. Bender? Bender!"

And on, the wall clock evidently stuck.

Question after question, like it's a Real-Nine-to-Five World Seminar and the world's a battle; if you don't enlist you're not in history; casualty rates, Antietam, Vietnam, corporations. Hate me, defile my yearbook photo, throw darts at it his tone says. But down the line, sessions later, when you've crawled through tape jungles, you'll think of your old prick C. O.

# 7

# A Minor Emergency

*A*nd if it's all wrecking me permanently well then okay, so what? There are worse things, like being born with two heads.

By the time the crosstown bus gets to Fifth Avenue I feel like I've got a hot rash all over. The bus is so crowded it almost tips over on the curves, squishing my face into the passengers on either side. A fat woman with two shopping bags over one forearm leans into me with the look of those who torture hamsters with live wires. I consider getting up for her but figure she's expecting me to and won't appreciate it if I do. She'll be reminded that she's a vicious fat woman without enough money to pay for cabfare being condescended to by a school kid and she'll resent me more. Better that she stand.

I take my tie over my head and stuff it into my schoolbag with my logoed school jacket, open the first few buttons of my shirt.

After the park the bus empties and the woman sits down in two seats across from me and does acupuncture on my kidneys all the way to Broadway.

Then she blocks my path off the bus, her whole body saying *You want to get ahead of me, don't you, don't you,* shaking with each step like an enormous warning finger made of jello, taking her time squishing through the bus door.

When I jump from the bus I jog the fifty yards through hard light to the pool room, bound the stairs.

In the grey light I see Gonzalez the dishwasher with his two hats one on top of the other shooting eight ball with Killer the ex-club middleweight who was hit in the throat too many times and starts every sentence with "eh eh eh." He showed me his scrapbook once, the yellowing clippings a chronicle of Catskill bloodbaths, fights sometimes only weeks a-part. Gonzalez never speaks; there's always such a vacant soap and steam smile on his face that it's hard to tell whether he's thinking or if he thinks at all.

"You talk too much," Freddie always says to him.

Nothing.

"Quiet now," Freddie says. "I've been here two minutes and you've said four hundred and seventeen words, okay. I'm clocking you. You don't stop talking."

Silence.

"Gonzalez, I'm going to put a fucking lock on your mouth if you can't keep it shut. I mean it. You give me a headache."

And Gonzalez just looks at him with that smile.

Rebel has a tropical fish on the line and will reel in every cent the man has. I wander along the wall and sit down where I can watch him sandbagging, coffee-housing around the table, looking good enough to hide that he's great, his fat fingers soft around a delicate cue, the stroke short and lethal, but his sad dog eyes implore me not to mess psychically with his action. He believes in karma and fields of brain waves and is always paranoid someone's going to spook his suckers.

"Shoot some?" says a gypsy with cartoon bulging biceps, who wears about eight colored handkerchiefs, as if someone tacked a trick handkerchief to his neck and spun him. His voice is oddly small for his body, faint and babyish, almost shy.

"What for?" I say.

"Couple three bucks, maybe?"

"What game?"

"Six ball, okay?"

"Sure, okay, get the balls," I say.

Hard to resist candy. I put the one through the five at the top of the rack and add the nine as money ball.

He's just decent enough with the cue not to sense when he's beat and just enough of a pineapple-upsidedown cake for me to string along, knowing it's getting time to go home but feeling the control deliciously rich, cruel and thrilling. He pockets okay but never does anything sane with the cue ball twice in a row, pool-stupid, like racking the balls odd-even for eight ball would be a Rubic's cube for him; always at the crucial point he freezes in a way that lets me win without showing much, until he's elbow deep into his jeans pockets. I make a good cut shot to win, then two hard cross-banks and he collapses, starts shooting fast, utterly nuts in his shot selection, the rack over his shoulder as he shoots, unable to make a ball anymore

61

so that he might as well pay me and have done. Something tells me to ease up because he's so badly busted and hopeless but I keep thinking the only way out now is to free-stroke through him, take no prisoners, make my contribution to clarity.

But when things get clear to him he comes around the table as if to pay and seizes me, lifting me onto my toes, scrunching my shirt in one hand into a hardball while with the other he brings a switchblade flat against the glands below my left jawbone, moving my head up until I have to face him. The feel of the metal, cold and sharp, brings sudden lucidity. I watch a bead of sweat zigging a course down his face, then another zagging his forehead, over the fat pocked nose, fast down the cheek. He looks about to explode and I'm scared if I move too fast he'll have my head swinging off my shoulders like a door on a hinge. Cautiously, I start dribbling clumps of singles and fives out of my pockets until there's a little heap on the table. Some of the local kids draw around, laughing at the rich white boy, scared with his book bag by the window, looking at the money like hyenas. Gypsy could cut my throat and they'd lap the blood.

"Pocket the bills," Gypsy says, quietly. "I want to win them back."

"Okay," I say, and we raise the stakes and he starts winning his money back, me being careful not to let it look too easy, but wanting to get it over, arranging to lose every game.

Half what I'd won gone, Scorpio appears.

He watches for a minute, his eyes narrowing. There's a flash in his eyes like his mind has photographed the scene and developed what's happening. He's wearing an Hawaiian shirt that's blue with red and yellow birds flying all over it and a white dinner jacket.

I dog the five ball and Gypsy double banks it and winds up straight on the nine.

"You no shooting so good," Scorpio says to me.

I can't say anything, can't even look at him. The look in his face nauseates me, makes me want to crawl under the table.

"Whatsa matter with you, kyyd?" he says. "You no feeling good you quit. But you play your game and you supposed to eat this gypsy fish."

So I get serious again. Gypsy's playing loose and cocky, slapping at the balls and playing wild combinations, and I bear down and start running him off the table. He doesn't catch on until I've done it three times straight.

Then he comes at me with his stick held the wrong way around and almost on its own my arm shoots out and finds his nose, the shock coursing my hand. Blood streams from one of his nostrils and he lifts me right off the ground by the hair and socks me a shot to the belly as I swing into him, dangling, my scalp on fire.

Then he's clear away and Scorpio and him roll once, Scorpio springing up quick. I can still hardly believe I hit Gypsy; my hand throbs disbelief.

"I no want no trouble," Scorpio says. "I no want no trouble with you, but you no touch this kyyd. Understand?"

A couple of the local kids mill around the table

when they see Roger coming from behind the counter with an aluminum baseball bat. He's got huge arms and walks with the thing like he's bored.

"Ya'll cut this shit," he says, "or's gonna be home run derby around here."

Gypsy looks at me, panting with hate, his blood on my face and shirt.

"Ya'll cut it now," Roger says, making on-deck circle motions with the bat.

My scalp burns and I feel for blood or premature bald spots.

"Get out of here, Gypsy," Roger says. "You barred. Don't let me see your ass around here no more now."

"Fuck this place anyway," Gypsy says, spits on the floor.

"Chipmunk," Roger says when he's gone. "What the hell's wrong with you? Don't you have no sense in you? White boy's supposed to have a little sense. Bring me those balls."

"Come on, Rodge."

"I ought to let that fucker kill your stinking white ass."

He looks at Scorpio who's running a thin comb through his hair, straightening out his shirt.

"Think you always gonna have someone to come to your fucking rescue?"

And he walks off mumbling, "Work's too hard, don't get paid for this shit, got to let those suckers kill each other."

I'm still rubbing my head, trying not to let anyone see the shake through my shoulders, tremor in my hands.

"Oh shit, he picked you up by your hair," one of the kids says, doubling with laughter.

"Thanks," I say to Scorpio. "Thanks for helping me out."

"Don't never let no one push you around, kyyd," Scorpio says. "Shoot your game, kyyd. You got a game. Stupid fucking gypsy."

# 8

# The Courts

*M*orning a grey glow, sun not up but the air already thick, we get to the courts before anyone's there but the few bums sprawled on benches outside the fence. There are four half courts and a full court with nets sewn on for summer tournaments. The lines and foul lanes have been freshly painted yellow against the smooth ashphalt. George does full court lay-ups while the rest of us lace tight our cons. We start with Dad and George against me and Hank, though later we shuffle the teams. We always play without keeping score, but any time one side gets ahead, moves with the happy automatic swagger that suggests lopsidedness, the other gets silent, perceptibly more serious.

Hank is tallest and can go inside when he gets pissed off. He doesn't do it much because he loses in that it's unsporting, but it's also a way of rubbing in the facts of life, our respective positions, the Real World of basketball, the game stacked against the small man, who has to find a way to survive. When Hank backs in I fake one way and go to the other, trying to keep him off balance and go for the steal, but once he gets my rhythm, learns to feel me sliding into overplays, it's pretty hard to get around him, borderline hopeless. He backs in with the ball out on a long dribble and then hits short hook shots or turn-around jumpers. I find myself wanting him to miss fiercely, incredibly aggressive after the loose balls, pressing the tempo, swinging the pass and circling the baseline so he'll get tired and slack, trying to push the game to where the legs get dead and the mind turns off and it's mostly heart and hustle and one of us has to give.

I could try backing in on George, who's even shorter than I am, but never do, partly because I've never developed an inside game, having always played point guard, been the designated press and zone buster, and my game's an assortment of scoops, slips between picks, running bank hook shots, quick chest-high jumpers off the dribble, hard cuts. Find the seam, penetrate, dish off.

But mostly I don't post on George because I know how much it hurts. Every gym class for the past five winters I've had to cover some towering stone-handed stiff who can back in on me and fumble the ball up against the backboard until something drops. In a full-court game, at the top of the zone, I'm protected, but even then there's usually something to remind me. I remember on the foul line of a J. V. game hearing a girl yell, "Isn't it a little late for you to be out?" and the hilarious rolling laughter. "Isn't it past your bed time, small fry?" And I actually took a step off the line and looked at the girl, sickening when

I saw how unattainably pretty she was, her breasts swelling a tight sweater.

"Hey small fry, hey small fry," the girl yelled. "Oh you're so cute."

"Don't listen to that shit, let's get two," said Al, our rebounding forward, from a foot above.

But when one gym class the guys were trying dunks and I said that I'd jam it backwards when I reached five-foot ten, even Al couldn't hide his amused sympathy, find an easy hilarity. The idea of me reaching such heights was beyond laughter.

After about an hour of non-stop ball we're all drenched and Dad has to take a breather because he's not in the shape he used to be. We've been brought up on Army basketball stories and can always feel that it bugs him to be a step slower, to be the one resorting to the marginally legal pick game and finally blowing the whistle, but that he's accepted where he is and doesn't want to be another heart statistic like a college roommate of his who dropped dead on a tennis court. Dead to his wife and three kids. Dad's got a solidity around the middle bordering on a gut, thirty pounds over his playing days. In the family album there's a picture of him driving to the hoop surrounded by guys with Kansas haircuts, and one of him with pinched post-game cheeks, happy exhaustion and a trophy. When we sit by the fence his knees crack and he loosens the laces of his shoes, socks hanging down to the edges of taped ankles. We try not to seem spry, but George can't help it, hits Dad up for a few bucks and darts off for sodas and ice cream from Hal the vendor who's set up in front of the playground next to the courts for years. By now a few other courts are going and we sit in silence, listening to the uneven thuds of the balls bouncing, drinking the sodas, the mid-May sun beginning to cut through the smog and heat the asphalt.

"Want to talk to you, Andy," Dad says. "Let's go sit on the bench."

"Sure, Dad," I say.

We sit under overhanging oak trees outside the wire fence that runs around the courts. The oak's bark is peeling and sickly looking, as if the tree has leprosy. Several locals bike by with arms out long for flying high-fives. Dad's quiet, brooding, his pale blue eyes full of a look I saw once when I surprised him at the office—a look of patient suffering before the thankless task of a desk piled high with scientific reports, print-outs, mechanicals, demo models, all to be smoothed into the glossy pages of *Global Refrigerator, GlassWorks* and whatever trade magazines he was editing that month, a look which said I'm up to the gills in all of this and you're farting your life away. Silence lays the heaviest guilt trip. Now he's winding up for a speech I hope won't embarrass us both.

"You're playing too much pool," he says. "It's wrecking your jump shot."

Oh that's beautiful, a masterful opening.

I can't contain a broad smile.

"My jumper's okay, Dad," I say.

"A little flat. You should put more spin on it." He demonstrates the right wrist action, leans back, then inches in for what he's planned to say.

"I could use a little help from you around the house." I nod.

"Meaning what?"

"Meaning you miss dinners without calling and get in at five in the morning. I'm not an idiot. You say you're going places when you're not and then run off to the pool room and it's disrupting everyone's life."

I try to think how he's caught me lying. I know he's referring to specific events but is too tidy to reveal his sources. I can't really suspect George, whose mind works so much like mine, and to whom I've done nothing abusive lately. Anyway, it doesn't matter much. I have to say something.

"Are you asking me to quit pool or cut back?" I say, with too much throat in my voice.

"You're too old for me to tell you what to do," he says. "You'll be away at college soon. You can do what you want then."

I'm not sure how to play this; when I don't volunteer any defense or concession he asks: "Could you quit? Have you thought about whether you are in control?"

"I haven't thought about it that much."

Would that mean I'm in or out of control? If you think you are out of control mightn't that be a kind of control? And for that matter, doesn't everyone think they're under control? As the Greeks say: Examine the mind of a Turk you find a field of thorns, examine the mind of a Greek you find harmony.

I make like I'm emerging from deep thought.

"Don't be a smart ass with me, Andy," Dad says. "I'm not some old square."

"I'm sorry, Dad."

"It's easy to say you're sorry, Andy."

"Of course I'm in control, Dad," I say. "And yes I could quit."

But even as I speak there's a stab of uneasiness. Sure, I can quit—anyone *can* quit anything—lock himself in a room full of Holy Books. But even locked up I'd love the game as much—and why shouldn't I?—still feel the blood rush around the table, the physical response to the green. If they make all the tables orange I'll get it all out of my system, but as long as they're green. . . .

I see the big black guy with thick-lensed glasses Sweats called Buddha circling the table, body ducking slightly over the table, bridge hand stationing the soft dips of his cue stick, and I see Scorpio in the shadows watching him intensely, even riveted, and paying him almost every game.

At first it's hard, even in memory, to see just how good the man is, because he never takes a hard shot. It's all so ordinary; the cue ball hardly moves; the balls just seem to line up, game after game, sequence after sequence, until the plainness appears cold precision, devoid of any feeling, until watching hurts.

"Who's that guy Scorpio's shooting?" I asked.

"That's the fucking Buddha himself," Freddie said. "The guy ain't too good. He's three good."

"Four good," Panama said, sick to see Scorpio so outclassed.

"I call him fucking Buddha because he never says

nothing," Freddie said. "It's like he's so fucking at peace with himself."

Yeah, I'll quit for ten years, and when I come back sometime in someplace seedy, wearing a monkey suit on the road or getting plastered alone in a bar, I'll come back, the tables won't surprise me. I'll pick up a stick, roll it over the table for straightness, powder my hands and know what to do. I'll take it all slowly. It'll all come back.

"Look," Dad says. "No lectures, just try to keep things in proportion."

# 9

# The Night Cafe

*I*t's slow for a few weeks. Most of the regulars are hard money until the welfare checks come. They play tight as if every shot they miss is a forkful of takeout Chinese yanked from in front of their mouths, kung pao chicken on a string. When I move to get a rack of balls to play Gonzalez, Freddie the Fish practically breaks his neck shaking his head.

"Ask to see his money, kid," Freddie says. "That's the brokest sucker alive. First of the month you play him."

And Freddie makes a motion like dogs humping, swaying his whole body and throwing his shoulders back.

"First of the month you put it to him, kid, know what I'm saying to you?"

"I hear you, Freddie."

And he's right. If you don't collect you didn't win. On the first Gonzalez will walk with a lift and a light in his face, like a fat man wearing a lobster-decorated plastic bib moving for a seafood smorgasbord, like he's loaded.

"Got a few dollars I can hold until next week, kid?"
Freddie says.

"Sure Freddie."

"Thanks, kid."

"Anytime, Freddie."

"Stay out of this, don't talk so much," Freddie says
to Gonzalez, whose eyes follow my five dollars into
Freddie's palm, watching like he's recording some
exchange of state secrets.

"Gonzalez, speak only when spoken to. House
man, make Gonzalez stop talking. Put a cork in his
mouth. The man makes me crazy with his chattering."

With my head on my desk I shoot on this three-
dimensional table, the paths of the balls leaving traces
of colored lazer light, balls slicing up and down, held
in place by a flourescent green medium thick enough
to support what has not been stricken into motion.
Scorpio's cross-bank rolls through it from corner to
corner, the cue ball swapping places magically with
the nine, rolling from pocket to pocket across my
open notebook between slides in the dark of Art
History, Dr. Reizen's lit pointer like a cue stick:

"After 1860 Courbet's subject matter becomes more
sensuous and luminous, the emphasis less on doc-
trinaire realism or statement, the colors more glowing
and resonant with life."

A slide of two naked women in sleepy embrace fills
the screen, their legs so tangled it's hard to see whose
are whose; the room's suddenly quiet. Reizen's stick
circles a painted vase overflowing with bright flowers:

"His backdrops are now more exotic, arabesque, here almost oriental."

The stick circles a cluster of blue-tinted vases on an enamelled desk and a string of pearls on the rumpled bed:

"The heads of the women are thrown back in the aspect of sensuous pleasure; every detail contributes to the sensuousness of the scene; the hair receives special attention—note that one's is black and resplendent like a pillow cushioning her head while the other's catches the light, warm in cascading tresses."

There's a quaver in his voice as he repeats "sensuous," like he's a hardon opening a plasticated magazine, and as he runs the pointer along the lines of the hair he brushes one woman's breast so that all of us shift in our seats with a faint titter. All I can look at is the one's pink lips almost parted and maybe an inch from the other's pink standing nipple.

"Who do you like better?" Jonesy whispers.

"What?"

"Who do you think's hotter?"

"The brunette," I say.

"Yeah, she's hot. The blonde's not bad either."

Jonesy can't think of much besides women these days—all subjects lead around to who's curvaceous, stacked, hot; who puts out and who's a tease.

Between classes we pitch quarters against the hallway walls, swapping stories, Jonesy talking with a swagger about his love life.

"Throw your coin away, Jonesy," Joe says.

"Take my money," Jonesy says, his good-natured

face beaming as his coin bangs against the wall and rolls out.

Jonesy's long hair is bound in back with a rubber band.

"What is it with the pony tail, Jonesy?" I ask him. "You look like Christopher Columbus."

"I figure," he says as I step to the line, bend at the knees, and toss the coin on a low flat angle. "I figure," he says, "my time's an investment. If I talk with a girl twenty minutes I got to come away with her phone number. If I walk five blocks I want a kiss goodnight, ten blocks and I'm into her shirt, any more than that and I'm heading for Palm Springs. . . ."

"What if you don't get shit?" Mike says, as I scoop up their quarters, my pocket starting to bulge like an arcade attendant's.

"Futurities," Jonesy says. "You got to believe in Futurities."

Reizen flashes through Manet, Monet, and is onto Van Gogh, my head as flat on the desk as dropped clay when I hear "billiard table" and look up and see a man in a white suit frozen in front of a table, lovers drunk in the background, foreheads kissing through a drunken haze, wine bottles, and in the center a rhombus of green, all uneven but right, the way a table looks from an angle at table level, and that man with a cue who seems to say, "It's late and I'm alone and here to shoot a few with anyone willing at this hour to help wipe off the filth of one world with the filth of another, take five on the run, shoot some?" And when Reizen flashes on to Gauguin and tanned tropical nudes and Cezanne and some fairly hefty nudes, and then some stuff that if painted on buildings would be

78

considered defacement of property, I still see those three balls from "The Night Cafe" and fantasize how I'd make the shot, caroming around, touching three cushions so the balls don't kiss, the white ball clicking against the red and all three rolling into place, men laying their bets, bills strewn over the green like salt on the pan at pay-up time, Panama by the man in white, now snapping his fingers after the dice, dice leaping over the pool balls: "Hey neena, sweet neena, how many lives does a cat have, show em, neena."

I go to a lot of parties, mostly because they give me good cover, make it easier to slip out again into the night, the moon ducking across a slate sky and my pace increasing, physically incapable of so much as detouring for pepperoni pizza, the vitamin S of a monster chocolate chip cookie, the high buildings rising around and guiding me like an extended awning to the steps of Guys and Dolls pool room.

# 10

# The Matchmaker

*M*ost afternoons I practice on the corner table by the window, as far away from the main action as I can, setting up shots and putting a piece of notebook paper on the table and trying to pocket the object ball and bring the cue ball to rest on the paper. Position for the next shot, pocket and position, a deep soothing sweetness when the slowing cue ball dies on the paper. Never just after the object ball; pocket and do more. I try it from different positions, always looking to do it the simplest way, move and create, and the time gets lost. Only a sudden weariness makes me look up at the clock, find myself covered with sweat.

I'm working on killing the cue ball after cut shots when I sense someone and look up.

"You getting better, kyyd," Scorpio says. "You practicing?"

"Yeah, killing some time."

"I no practice no more," he says.

I'm going to tell him he doesn't need it, that I wouldn't practice if I could shoot like him, but it's a lie and would sound stupid, not mean anything to him. In a way I'm sorry he doesn't practice. There's something nice about imagining him alone in a room late at night working on complicated positions. But then I see the rightness of his not practicing—just making great shots in the great moments—like creativity's a thing in the blood to be discovered on the last ball, in an action that counts for something.

"You gotta girl, kyyd?" Scorpio asks.

"No one in particular," I say, and pocket another ball.

Dad always asks Hank, who's had a steady stream of air-heads blowing across his life before Mindy, whether there is *anyone in particular* he likes, which always gets a roll of the eyes out of Sarah and George.

"That's bad, man," Scorpio says, looking serious, thinking for a minute.

"What?" I say.

"That you no getting any."

"I do okay for myself," I say.

Actually, the last girl I kissed was Eileen, probably a month ago at a party, until my tongue was practically sprained, and I've never been much past kissing. The girl I liked through elementary school, named of all things Betsy, started sleeping around when we were in ninth grade and it stings against my will to see her with big dumb-ass guys just because they have hair on their chests. I'm not sure I like her anymore, whether it's just the idea of her, or just being excluded from her. We talk so little I could say I made her up if there weren't so many football players who'd swear to her existence. At the prom she wore one of those gauzy dresses that reveals more than it hides and her dancing was fantastically bad, as if she were purposely misusing the music, opposing it with herself. I sat alone in a ridiculous white Great Gatsby suit handed down from Hank watching everyone paired up and dancing while I downed a pint of Henessey, my eyes scotch-taped to Betsy's bosom, which remained unaware upon its bearer of my demand or presence, looking at Betsy's plumpening form when the light assisted, wondering how I could still think about this girl I'd held hands with behind a bush during recess in fifth grade but who'd been nothing but amused by me for years—"You could always make me laugh," she said to me at one party.

"Like to dance with me, Andy?" Francine says, and I say, "Sure, Henessey," and am half way across the floor trying to find my dancing legs before I realize I've addressed her as a cognac.

"Hey," Scorpio says. "What you doing tomorrow night?"

"Dunno," I say.

"You coming around here, maybe?"

"Yeah, I might be up here."

"Cause you could help me out, do me a favor."

"Sure," I say.

"See, cause this lady I'm seeing. She got a little sister. I think you like her."

"How little?" I say.

Scorpio laughs in a way that scares me a little, that sounds unhealthy, like he's been inhaling bus fumes straight from the exhaust. He shakes with laughter and wipes his hand across his face.

"Kyyd, you very funny, you kill me. Man, you like this girl, she make you shoot better."

"Shit," I say.

"I no fooling you," Scorpio says, seriousness edged into his voice, like he means it. "She fix your whole game up, loosen your stroke."

He comes off the wall and chops a few of the balls around with his hands, then uses a ball in his fist like a cue ball.

"Man, do me a favor." He laughs. "Whatsa matter, you no like the ladies, you a faggot?"

"Course I like girls," I say.

"You sure, cause you no like . . ."

"Don't worry."

"You sure you not like a three-dollar bill?"

"More like a C-note."

"That's good, kid, that's good. So I pick you up here around nine."

I try to say something but he waves me quiet.

"You no here you not my friend."

"Okay, okay," I say.

"Look, maybe you dress a little more normal like, you know, you put on a jacket, a nice shirt with a design on it maybe, comb your hair a little, make yourself look nice."

# 11

# Of Dying Men

*S*ometimes I think tipping street-flutists or helping blind men over curbs on a regular basis aids one's good fortune. Probably, though, it's illogical to think of the gambling gods and the Boy Scout, Good-Humor truck, apple pie, pawn-to-king-four, gold-standard, missionary position ones rewarding similar deeds. Around the house I feel I'm racking up good points for being polite or studious—that if I give proof that I'm not totally fucked up there will be less psychic opposition.

When Mom gets home I'm reading on the living room rug with papers, books, notecards strewn about and a clip board conspicuously cluttered with hacked sentences. Hank has taken George and Sarah to an afternoon movie. Dad's running about half an hour late so Mom and I walk slowly toward Broadway to meet him for dinner.

"I worry about you and those people," Mom says, while we're waiting to cross West End Avenue, her tone light but with a concern that can't wait until the light changes.

"They don't bite, Mom," I say. "You shouldn't worry so much, Mom."

"I know, it's just that they keep themselves dirty and low."

"And position's nine-tenths of the law?"

"They're hollow people. They lead twisted, empty lives. You don't want to end up that way."

"I don't suppose anyone actively attempts to be twisted, hollow, and empty, Mom," I say.

"No," Mom says, with a laugh. "Not actively."

"What's really bugging you? Is it that I'm going to a college that's listed 'very' and not 'most competitive?' "

"That's not fair, Andy. No one's ever said that."

"But you've felt it."

"Okay, so what. You could have gone anywhere if you'd worked more, but you'll do well when you want to."

"I appreciate your confidence, Mom. Thanks."

Mom stops with her hands on her hips.

"Peace, okay," she says, finally, and we shake on it. "How about a play this week, a play and dinner. I'll get tickets for 'Cats.' "

"Sounds good," I say, thinking of Bean rubbing his shoulders against the cue racks and purring to himself. "Let's see, I have a date with a degenerate on Thursday and a conference with a bag lady on Tuesday. Is Wednesday night fine with you?"

"Wednesday's fine."

"Great. How's Spaghetti-Os coming?"

"Okay, I guess. Tell me what you think of this?"

And she takes a sketch pad out of her purse and flips

86

to a hearty Italian couple beaming over a great steaming bowl of Spaghetti-Os, cows and other creatures of the field in the background.

"You'll put the restaurants out of business," I say.

We eat at one of those places families go to after funerals or graduations. The ceiling is all misty mirror and because the lights are so low and the candles in the center of each table are round and bright, the place looks like a convention of seancers. Flickering light moves over the contours of Dad's lower face, making great puddles of shadow around his eyes.

For the past two summers I've bussed tables so during time-outs in our discussion about liberalism versus socialism, whether one has an obligation to help the dying man in the street or a right not to help him, I clock the busboys. Ours is good, a little lax on silverware, loud, an occasional clatter, but technically sound, understanding the dishes well and not interfering with the flow of our meal. In a few weeks school ends and I'll be back in the restaurant, cruising the floor for empty dishes, wiping down the laminated mahogany tables. Mom thinks you've got to help that dying man in the street, that it's inhuman not to; Dad says that personally he would if he could, but that he respects a person's freedom not to, that to force one to live one's life for others is as bad as not caring about suffering. I argue that there is no hypothetical "dying man" in the street but different real men which means every situation's different and sometimes it's right and possible to help and at other times helping's inadvisable or one doesn't know how or the dying man in the street doesn't want help, and I tell them about this sociological study done on an order of Good Samaritans in which thirty-eight good Samaritans were sent to this meeting on charity and helping the homeless and had to walk through a hallway in which a ragged man implored each of them for assistance. An undercover bum; only one Samaritan stopped.

"Helping others can be about liking yourself," I say.

Mom glowers at me. "Hey, I thought we signed a treaty?"

Dad and Mom talk paste-ups and circulation for a few minutes, exchanging office reports, their ritual, or politeness. Dad's watch says it's two hours before I'm supposed to meet Scorpio and I start playing out date scenarios, me providing the solution to the latino mystery of slow foot in a rhumba club. Nothing inviting. Types of faces and figures scroll rapidly through my head including the usual date with a seeing-eye dog until Mom asks whether I've got any plans for the night, a question interpretable, I suppose, as joke.

"I'm going out tonight," I say, loving how the vagueness will make them instantly convict me and will set them up to later stew in the recognition of their own imperfect perceptive faculties.

"Going to see your pals at the pool room?" Mom asks, rushing at the bait.

"Yes," I say. "A colleague and I are meeting two ladies there."

I wonder whether Scorpio will in fact bring the women up to the pool room. A little doubles eight ball wouldn't be so bad. Reaching around my date's tapering waist to guide her cue stick: *Softly now, easy, line it up, right, like that,* and *Which ball should I go for? Like this? This way?*

"And then you are going to the opera?" Mom says.

"Actually, we *are* planning a cultural evening," I say.

"Oh Andy," Mom says, breaking down. "When are you going to stop all these games?"

"I'm not dying in the street yet, Mom," I say.

"Andy. . . ."

"Oh please pass the calamine lotion, Mother dear."

"Okay," Dad says. "We're having a nice meal. I'm enjoying my lasagna and you're enjoying your shrimp and Andy's ravioli looks. . . ."


At home I go to Hank's room to borrow a jacket. He looks up from a desk littered with open books, making a point of lingering over some note in progress. Probably he's just writing Mindy, his girl of spandex jogging tights and hair-curling kits, and has the books out to pepper his letter with cribbed love lyrics.

"What?" Hank says. "Jacket, yeah, sure, pick one out."

"Can I take this one?" I say, pointing to a shiny grey jacket.

He really doesn't want to lend it but senses I wouldn't ask him if I didn't care, and turns from his papers.

"Sure, just don't get anything on it," he says, with an older brotherly grin that slides into a getting-ready-to-give-creative-advice-from-my-well-of-worldly- experience look, but he can't proceed without an opening. I put the jacket on and since the sleeves are a few inches long roll them, the baggy look.

"Where are you going?"

"Date," I say, knowing the word is like an announcement over the family PA system and leaves open the possibility that this is part of a sequence of clandestine romances.

"Hey," Hank says. "Anyone I know?"

"I don't think so," I say. "Friend of a friend."

"That's good," he says, hesitating. "Well, have a good evening."

In the hallway Sarah whines to Mom that George has stolen her green tasseled scarf and says he's going to wear it to school.

"It'll look very funny on him, won't it," Mom says. "All his friends will laugh at him."

"I don't want people laughing at my brother," Sarah says. "And I want my scarf back."

# 12

# Variations in Riverside Park

*S*corpio shows up a few minutes after nine with his cat step, head swiveling to take in the action out of habit, jaw working, wearing a tight black body shirt, black pants and white shoes.

"You looking pretty sharp tonight, kyyd," he says, taking in the jacket.

"Thanks," I say. "You too."

I'm standing on the edge of the player area watching Killer and String Bean play eight ball. When Bean makes a good shot he hop skips his great body over to the wall, light on his feet, and rubs his shoulders and his head against it and purrs, "Oh you shoots so good, oh baby you shoots so good, oh baby . . ." and Killer just stands by the table mumbling "eh eh eh," shaking his head and shrugging periodically, fishing around in his pocket for payment, eyes bulging like an electrocuted frog's.

Scorpio goes to the phone booth and makes a call. Robby asks me to play twice and I turn him down—never liked his action anyway, kind of guy who talks too much with this thick marijuana accent, shoots fast and straight for a little while, exaggerating the draw, until the pockets tighten on him.

"What's wrong, kid, you broke?"

"I'm never broke," I say. "I don't leave home without it."

"You play me you be broke," he says. "That's hundred percent fact. You be so broke you don't know what to do."

"If you shoot real good for a real long time maybe I'll start getting broke," I say.

"Just don't quit til I get it all," Robby says.

Scorpio comes back and looks at me like I'm pitiful.

"Come on kyyd, you shoot pool later, we got ladies waiting."

"Oh, ladies," Robby says, sculpting an ass with his hands in the air. "That's why you fraid to play me."

"Shut up," Scorpio says.

"Eat me," Robby says.

"You ain't got no dick to eat," Scorpio says.

"What's this?" Robby says, dropping his pants.

Scorpio looks him over, frowning.

"It's a fake," he says, finally. "It's made out of rubber."

And we're out on the street moving downtown.

"Now you gotta be polite to her," Scorpio says. "Show her some respect."

"Don't worry," I say.

Is he serious? What does he think I'll do to her?

I walk along thinking, *This is a mistake, what am I getting into, look who's handing me soapbox lectures about*

92

respect, *a guy who I saw go into the bathroom with a hooker who takes checks for God only knows what sort of carnal favors . . . this little sister's probably gonna give me some rare tropical Puerto Rican spotted fever just by breathing on me, I'm going to have to swing upsidedown from a chinning bar to take a piss . . . man o man, all I wanna do is play pool and gamble, find a nice clean table and a peaceful sucker and stay out of trouble.*

"She's a nice girl," Scorpio says. "You like her."

"I'm sure I will," I say, trying to look like this is all routine to me, like taking welfare checks off suckers on lazy start-of-the-month afternoons.

What the fuck am I supposed to say to this girl anyway?

*Shit,* I hear Jonesy say. *If you want educated conversation turn on PBS.*

The ladies are waiting in front of Ernie's restaurant. I've barely time to take them in before Scorpio's woman says "You're late" and Scorpio makes a quick move and kisses her on both cheeks, then longer on the lips.

"I know, baby, I'm sorry."

"You're always late and you're always sorry," she says, straightening out a red dress so tight I'm surprised it can wrinkle.

"Yeah," he says. "Kyyd, this is my main lady Laura and this is her sister Maria."

"Hi," Maria says. She's got a slightly dazzled look on her face, a kind of ripe plastic innocence, lips so candy red I want to check for a wrapper, and she's carrying one of those stylish square leather purses that looks like a lunch box.

93

"Has the kid got a name?" Laura asks Scorpio.

"Andy," I say.

"Andy," Scorpio says.

"Hello, Andy," she says nicely, shakes my hand. "You play pool too."

"Now and then."

"I'll bet."

"Come on," Scorpio says. "Let's get out of the sidewalk, sit down some place."

We drink two rounds of pina coladas in a place where slanting mirrors catch and play with the light and Victorian nudes coax and beckon from lavender walls; each breast small, garnished with a single flower. Scorpio and Laura hold hands and talk softly in Spanish.

Maria says she is in tenth grade at a public school I've never heard of and has two other sisters besides Laura and likes to drink and loves to listen to music and go dancing. She doesn't look a minute out of eighth grade, but I don't look a minute out of ninth. Since I don't know anything about music, though I like to listen to just about anything, I steer the talk toward her family, get her going about her relationships with her sisters. She and Laura are closest; the other two are more like mothers. One's been married twice and abandoned twice and now lives at home with her two-year-old kid. I tell her I have a little sister who's hard to see right now as more than just my little sister.

"I never know exactly what to talk about with her,"

94

I say. "I don't know how to find things to do and don't want to treat her like she's a baby."

"But you love her, right?" Maria says.

"Of course I do."

"And that's what's important, right?"

"Yes," I say.

"What does she look like?"

"Frizzy hair, lots of freckles. . . ."

"Runs in the family."

And so forth.

At first Maria doesn't look at me when she talks, but on the second colada she does, and when I speak about Sarah she looks at me with almost too much concern, eyebrows contorted by concentration, as if anything I say might make a tremendous difference for the next five minutes. When she moves her glass to her mouth she lips the rim, guiding the smallest sips into her mouth with her tongue. I start getting lulled by her eyes, which are part green and flecked with red, and leave off listening closely or thinking about what she says.

Outside the restaurant Scorpio palms a Trojan into my hand, winks at me. I put the thing in Hank's baggy jacket pocket, shaking my head. We walk down by the waist-high stone fence of Riverside Drive and enter the park at Eighty-third Street, Laura and Scorpio ahead of us melded together like Siamese twins.

I put my arm around Maria and she snuggles up to me and I say *well* to myself, *well this is really unfair. I mean, decide whether you like this girl or not without any of*

95

*the extraneous stuff about whether you could take her home and introduce her to your friends or are you supposed to break out singing "I just met a girl named Maria."* And then I think all the social stuff's mooseshit and the real point is whether I'm scared to try to get her clothes off, isn't it? Find out what it's all about with that Trojan, learn in the park, doing it in the dark, with a girl I don't know. Just sex as it should be the first time so that if my turn ever comes with a Real Betsy I'll know what to do, because it's stupid to walk around not knowing what to do when learning's so easy. Totally selfish shit, yes. But a little realism never hurts.

"You're a funny guy," she says, and I turn with a sudden terror that she's been reading my thoughts.

"Am I? Why so funny?"

She mouths something.

"What?" I say.

"Read my lips."

And when I look at those lips I give a spasmodic shiver I have to extend into a stretch.

"Are you sore," she says.

"Nothing, just a kink," I say.

"You're not a kinky guy, are you?" she says, and we laugh at her little joke.

"Not usually," I say, looking at her again and feeling a sudden desire to please and excite her. "But why am I so funny?"

"You're just kind of funny, that's all. Kind of quiet."

"Good funny or bad funny?"

"Maybe good funny," she says, her head moving in

96

cute little shakes. "I don't know. It's like you don't want to show too much about yourself. I like you."

And she moves closer, her face smooth as polished china.

So it's my shot, kid.

I put my hand behind her head and we kiss. I open my eyes for a second and she's got her eyes closed. We kiss for maybe five minutes until there's a what-next feeling. When we come up for air I look around and don't see Scorpio.

"We could sit down," I say.

"Okay," she says.

We're near a bench about fifty yards from the park entrance but in the dark and we sit and start kissing again, her small tongue racing about my mouth. On the second kiss it's always more natural and I feel like I'm really with her.

I unbutton her shirt, untangling a little silver cross from between her third and fourth buttons and putting it over her head and down her back. She isn't wearing any bra and her breasts are small and hard like lemon halves, very marvelously rounded in my hands, her stomach unexpectedly hard, beyond firmness.

I begin to ask how she got so strong but she's unbuttoning my shirt now and running her hands around and over my stomach and waist until my whole body's crying *no no okay go ahead please* and she undoes my pants button and unzips the fly and takes me in hand, her hand so small and smooth, like it's been baby-powdered and I don't know what to do with my hands; first I put them on her shoulders, then after a minute lean my head back and look up at the stars feeling a welling up and then shivers of pleasure. A free wind blows across us both on the bench. I kiss her along the neck and ear, still tingling.

"That was nice," I say.

She nibbles on my ear.

"Do the same for me," she says.

And I start trying to figure how to get at her without removing the whole skirt, and am finally just lifting it when over her shoulder I make out a couple of dark forms moving slowing in a crouch-walk toward us, stopping behind the trees in the dog-doo field, then moving again. At first I think I'm imagining things but then I see one swing out from behind a tree and loop about ten paces to another one. I look for the other but have lost him.

"Maria," I whisper, all my senses alert. "I think we better get out of here now."

"Why?"

"Just come on. There's some guys out there."

Maria turns, her hair brushing my cheek, then turns back.

"Where?" she says. "I don't see anyone."

But she's hardly looked. She re-adjusts herself on my thighs with a sleepy slowness, one leg raised. I train my eyes into the darkness and now see them wheeling toward us across an open stretch where the grass has been worn away and looks oil-spill dark, just their dark torsoes moving as if on bicycles.

"Let's get out of here," I yell, grabbing her arm and starting for the park entrance, Maria in tow half-running and fumbling with the buttons of her shirt,

98

the lunch-box purse sliding over her shoulder, saying, "Wait, what, hey, Andy, what's wrong with you, where are you going Andy, slow down" and about twenty yards from the mouth of the park I look back and see the guys stop short and laugh, yell something after us, milling around.

"Shit," I say, breathing unbelievably hard.

Maria doesn't turn around, like she hasn't heard anything. She just stands there tucking in her shirt with no idea how close we were to being jumped, how close they were to her ass, a little sugar. She should be down on her knees praying to that cross that's slipped back between her breasts, but instead she's standing with her hands on her hips and an exasperated look.

# 13

# Antique Persians

*W*ith Buddha in my head I go back to the pool room.

Hilary and I are walking Broadway and when we near the brown awning I stop and look up at the long windows, now completely filled by rugs.

"How about let's have a look?" I say.

"Why so interested in rugs all of a sudden?" Hilary says.

"Didn't you know?" I say. "I've always been interested in rugs. I minored in Persian Rugs."

And why now? We've walked by this place a dozen times, and, though it's about five years since the Christmas break, when, home from school, I found it a rug shop, I've somehow never felt the desire to go up, or to talk with anyone about my pool days, as if pool were a used-to game, something done young, and the essence of good gambling's knowing when to pack it in, and no one could like or want much to do with my old gambling self, now that the edge, itch, draw, are gone.

When we've walked up through this neighborhood, passing Lincoln Center and the remodelled

Beacon, I've felt I was getting closer to something, but lacked any sense of disappointment when I passed it and went on. The whole neighborhood's changed in just the last few years; Zabars now stretches half a block, the pizza shop's gone, the movie theater now shows six movies, most of the greasy breakfast restaurants have become fancy boutiques or Oriental Fruit and Salad Bars, and the soot-darkened turn-of-the-century apartment buildings have been replaced by high-rise condominiums with Anglo-Ivy names like the Princeton or the Bromley. But somehow the feel, the pattern and quality of the streets remains.

Now I climb the familiar stairs slowly with Hilary, alongside a notched conveyor belt, surprised again at the cleanness of the stairwell, the soft carpeting and varnished wood bannisters, the clean white paint left ridged and caked like a topographical map. The chink in the wall at the top through which I used to talk with Roger has been widened into a neat open square with a potted crocus in it, ostensibly now less to keep out undesirables than to alert the stock-room boys in thigh-length tassled crimson shirts to get off their dolleys.

The feeling when I round the corner and face the room is not powerful but begins so deep that suddenly I know it's been in me, something buried and seeping out for a long time in installments, felt in deferred payments. There's a dull hollow feeling looking around, a faint fizzle in my limbs. Mostly what's gone is the light from the windows, which are covered with rugs; the room's now neon and bright as an office, lacking any sense of Broadway alive and

102

bustling below, pervaded by an odd humming silence.

I stand in the center of the room and turn slowly while Hilary wanders off and begins paging through the huge folios of rugs hanging from ceiling to floor from the rolling arms of metal rug racks. I turn and look at the rugs hanging where the cue racks once lined the walls; smaller Mexican blankets cover the wall where the old "No Gambling" signs hung, probably still there if anyone cared to look. When I turn I expect to see the room's old shape, smoke coiling upward in hanging lights, the green of the player table, side-betters shadowy against the wall. There's an eerie sense that I've stood in this same spot before, and in numerous spots now hidden by the rugs that ring the wall, moving each wall in about twenty feet so that the room feels tighter. So many nights I've walked home from here broke and hungry, imagining somebody eating a slow greasy breakfast with my cash, seeing so clearly the point when I should have quit, when I pulled the one more game and then another routine over my own eyes. So many mornings I've woken with this place in my head and a pool hangover, which, like a talking hangover or any other kind of hangover lasts half a day, after which I start in again, every time my eyes close seeing sequences, balls moving as if choreographed.

Maybe I've stood on exactly this spot betting my last five bucks, fighting off the shoots of weariness, heart racing, wanting nothing more than daylight for a run, a last chance to stave off incipient brokeness, find my groove and turn the night around, begin the

103

swing into parlay that no law of averages need end, free-stroking through rack after rack, the family, everything, distant, silver-grey.

Maybe I've stood on this spot watching String Bean and Killer Diller at one of their afternoon-long sessions of tactical eight ball, Bean rubbing his shoulders along the walls—*Oh baby, Oh baby*—Killer lowering his head over the table, bulging eyes switching like a tennis fan's from cue ball to object ball and back, lining his cue over a stiff open bridge, Sweats, the Manic Aggressive, worrying hard money on the side.

"Would you like to see any rug in particular, sir?" the owner says.

"No, no, I'm with her," I say, pointing to Hilary.

The room's mostly the same except for an addition in the corner where we used to play craps that's now some sort of show room with a space where a large cube of carpeting has been cut away to leave bare wood on which rugs are displayed. There's a strange effect of a rug lying wholly within but not part of another rug, hemmed around by a strip of wood, a one-dimensional Chinese box effect. Along the walls hang antique rugs, peacock feather extravagant and complex, only not bright, intricate with deep earthy dyes, purples and maroons, the absence of brightness, the muted colors, somehow moving.

I look at the tags:

Antique: Persian, Heriz, 12×18, very fine.
               Was 12,000, our reduced price, 8,000.
Antique: Isarta, Turkey, 14×18, fine. Was 9,000,
               our reduced price, 6,500.

"Andy, come and look at something," Hilary says, and takes me by the shirt and leads me across the room to where I used to practice on a corner table.

"Isn't it marvelous?" she says, folding the rack open to display a rug knotted exceptionally tight, purples and blacks and browns, thick and lovely.

Fereghan, Sarouk, 17 × 25, very fine. Was 50,000, our reduced price, 35,000.

"It's even on sale," I say. "There must be millions of dollars of rugs in here."

"Some of the others are Chinese art-deco, but this guy would go well in my living-room, don't you think?"

"Would you like it?"

"Yes, please," she says, with a look of such innocence a richer man might pull his checkbook and think later.

As we walk out followed by the owner I'm acutely aware that for me every part of this place has a meaning Hilary can't know about, brings back a time when I thought I only wanted to be great at something, that all kinds of greatness were connected, dishwashing, bussing tables, shooting one pocket, and I only wanted to touch some of it. When we near the counter I'm surprised to look up and not see Roger asking money for the time.

*Chipmunk, get your white ass out of here.*

*Lighten up, Roger.*

*How many times I got to explain shit to you, Chipmunk. Ain't you got no kind of sense at all?*

*Roger Roger. Get a Real Job.*

*Never. Work killed two of my uncles. Ain't gonna make that mistake.*

*Roger Roger.*

"The rugs are very beautiful," Hilary says to the man, flashing a prom-photo smile.

"Thank you," the rug man says with a little bow. "I hope you will hurry back to visit us."

# 14

# Columbus Avenue

*I* don't see Maria for about a week and then she comes up to the pool room in tasseled white leather boots and a white leather skirt and black T-shirt exposing a sliver of waist, looking like a character out of *Let's Go Long Island*. I'm practicing as usual in the corner and don't see her until she stands directly in my line of vision.

"Hey Maria," I say.

"Hi Andy," she says. "Who's winning?"

I pocket a ball.

"Too easy, show me something fancy."

I run the last three balls.

"Some other time. I've had enough. Time to quit."

"Come on," she says.

"My eyes are tired," I say, "Do you know how to give eyeball massage?"

I'm uncomfortable shooting with her watching; seeing clean women in the pool room always makes me feel dirty, suddenly aware of the chalk and dirt on my bridge hand, and when I practice I want to be alone without distractions, or with someone who sees what's being worked out.

I collect up the balls, thinking how to play this hand, what I want to happen, asking myself if her being there offering herself parsleyed on a platter makes her more or less appetizing.

"You look nice," I say, which I'd testify to under oath.

"Thank you," she says, still waiting a real move.

"How about a movie?" I ask.

"Okay," she says. "If you're not too busy."

I'm not sure how to take this, but it's generally best to leave space for irony.

"That your girlfriend?" Freddie says when I'm paying time.

"Nice fillie," he says to Roger, who answers with a grunt, but flashes a fat grin.

"Ya'll be good now, Chipmunk," Roger says, handing me the change.

"Maiden claiming, eh kid. Don't do nothing Roger wouldn't do," Freddie says, his hoarse laughter following us down the stairs.

Maria and I go to one of those movies that, four minutes after it starts, you wish is a preview, and goes on as if it is a preview for an hour and a half. One inane episode after another involving a California chemistry professor who experiments on his class, all parodically centerfoldish, Stepford rockettes—wrong potions get drunk, roles reversed, a kind of revenge of the Airheads. Maria laughs in a high giggle at the truly absurd scenes, when I'd have to tong my cheeks to hold a smile. I put my arm around her and she lays

108

her head against the crease between my neck and shoulder like a violin, her hair smelling clean and orangey.

We walk together holding hands and I can't help picturing what a summer would be like with her, a picnic in the park after work, a trip to Jones Beach, cotton candy and spreading Cocoa Butter on that hard little stomach. And then bye-bye, I'm off to college.

And why Maria?

Because she's available? So I can have a girlfriend? Someone to spend my spare time with? Because people have girlfriends and go out places together so they can feel better about themselves, more connected, wanted, needed? Because I could share my problems with her or learn more about sex?

I hate suddenly that there's not going to be conversation unless I start and control it, that we're going to make the kind of small talk that's pollution, and that I just want to be in the bathtub with her, hot and bubbly, somewhere naked with no words.

Should I say *I would like very much to take a bath with you?*

And if she has jasmine bubble bath in that square purse where will we go?

Wake George and ask him to sleep in the living room?

Ask Hank to borrow his room?

Make use of that nice hairy rug in the living room.

We have a few rounds at a bar on Columbus Avenue near where I'll begin work soon, and make short attempts at talk, broken by silence and stares that don't quite connect. I try a joke and when she doesn't pick up the irony and answers in a serious way I follow up as if I had been serious. The streets are already crowded: in a month there'll be mimes, the guys selling flourescent glow-in-the-dark sunglasses and earrings, the preacher with his bullhorn and placards hanging from both sides of him so that it looks like his head's sticking out of a shopping bag: "Sinners repent," he says into the bullhorn, voice a monotone. "Sinners repent, scientists are predicting a Major Earthquake in New York City. A May-Ger Earthquake in New York. Repent before it is too late." And it's the monotone that makes me see the earth splitting open under F. A. O. Schwartz, the skies raining stuffed cats and dogs, falling customers clutching for land, and a runaway express train routed for way downtown.

"In the summer there's a guy who stages turtle races out there," I tell Maria.

"Turtle races," she says. "Why?"

"I guess to make money."

"He must not make it very fast," she says.

I ask her how she liked the movie and she says she liked it okay. Her eyebrows vex into upsidedown vees; her lips, glossy red, curl down. It's starting to get late enough for her to see that I'm keeping everything out in the light.

"Don't you like me?" she asks.

"Of course I like you," I say.

"You know what I mean."

She holds her head at an angle like she's trying to figure me out, understand why we haven't made-out on a street corner like normal folks, why I haven't suggested a walk to some shady mugger-infested grove. I can't think what to say.

"I gotta go," she says. 'If I give you my number will you call me?"

"Sure," I say. "Can I walk you home?"

"I take the subway," she says.

"Want money for a cab?" I say. "I won some money today. Please."

"No," she says. "I like the subway. Give me a call sometime, okay?"

"I will."

"Okay, see you."

"Okay, Maria."

She leaves quickly, conscious of my eyes following her short quick step, firm legs. I watch with a surge of regret as she disappears down the avenue, consider running after her, amazed and sickened at the cowardice of what I've done, but order another round instead and sit back, twisted some, but also relieved. The booze lifts me up to where things are clear and sharp. The cafe bustles. "Aren't chairs wonderful things," a voice says behind me. On the sidewalk a guy's playing a harmonica solo that sounds like the sound track to a dog food commercial. I think about getting really plastered, so drunk I have to make it home on all fours, hugging trash cans, groping the sides of parked cars, staring at the doorman on West End Avenue and Eighty-Second Street like a dog, amazed to find anyone standing in front of a building in those clothes and that hat at that time of night. Already the streetlamps spread into the night like yellow watercolor dripped on a wet page. On the table in front of me on a pink piece of Snoopy notepad paper is the name Maria Ramirez and a number; I look at the neat rounded script with its dotted "i"s so hopeful and happy and turn it over in my hands, suddenly sure that I'll never call, probably never see her again, that it isn't in me to care about her enough to want to mix my life with hers, stomach full of emptiness and loathing for the retreating impulse in myself, full of longing for her, those fine thin eyelashes, flecked eyes, even as mere opportunity, but still approving the hard ugly finality. I pick up the Snoopy paper and consider leaving it somewhere in the house a little out of the way. Then I tear it slowly in half, pick up the halves and tear them in halves, and when her name is confetti I settle the check.

# 15

# Exit Scorpio

*T*he street at two a.m. on a night warm and thick, quiet except for the sandpapery sounds of garbage scratching across the pavement and leaves rustling at the tops of the scrawny trees planted at intervals and protected by knee-high brick boxes.

Scorpio and I walk for the pizza joint on Amsterdam and 75th. I've beat sixty dollars out of a junior exec at eight ball, and, awake and pumping, bet the side of Scorpio against Spanish Eddie, a downtown player, until Eddie gets a phone call and leaves. Scorpio explains a sequence to me, hands slicing the air, walking light and fast with the few hundred he's up, as if in a rush. He says I gotta have meatball lasagna and Dos Equis with him and then he's got to split for a date. I'm seeing the Dos Equis, amber, with a twist of lime wedged into the cold mouth of the bottle. The streets are unnaturally quiet, just Scorpio's voice, high and clipped, our quick footsteps and misshapen shadows beneath the yellow streetlights, smoke snaking from a manhole.

Then there's a car opening, men from two sides on

113

the street and a third pointing a gun, Scorpio tensing two moves ahead of me with a trapped-animal comprehension, eyes darting in all directions, limbs amazingly calm.

I'm still trying to size it.

"Be cool, kyyd," he whispers.

They ring in on him because it's him they're after and when I move closer and start to speak a man throws me with both hands into a car. I rise, shakily, pain through my shoulder and turn in his direction and thud, something slams the side of my face; there's sudden dizziness, a speeding up of forms and faces, then blankness. Moments glide past, and through a haze a car pulls away, screeches a corner, and again the street is empty and silent.

For minutes I lay back, straighten my legs, head spinning but no pain now. I lie there looking at the cloudless vaguely luminous grey sky between the buildings and want just to close my eyes. But then I look up and realize that I'm basically okay and lying on the sidewalk and must attempt to sit up, and when I'm sitting and brushing myself off I look around and it comes to me.

Scorpio.

Where's Scorpio?

Gone. And I've got to do something.

And I look around and all the dumpsters and the buildings and the parked cars are yelling and honking *Do something you fool. Don't just sit there, do something, anything but sit there.*

*Do something,* cries the pavement and *do something*

114

the parking meters and piles of corded newspapers, and just *for god's sake do something.*

Do what?

First, get up. Clear your head, think it through rationally, calmly. He's gone, don't know where, best to get help.

I run to the corner and call the cops and sit waiting for them on the curb punching my knuckles together with impatience and anger, feeling utterly useless, feeling there's got to be a better play I'm not finding. My head throbs and I can feel my eyebrow and cheek closing in on each other with a pulsing, rising dullness. A man passes and asks if I'm okay and do I need help and moves on. By the time the cops show Scorpio might be in a meat-packing plant in Jersey.

"Looks like you lost the fight," one says, getting out of the car.

I tell him I'm okay and about Scorpio.

"Where'd this happen?"

"Middle of the block."

"Take us there."

We look around, nothing. I don't know what we're looking for, what we could possibly find. Clues? He puts his hand on his hips, scratches his moustache, moving heavy and slow.

"Yup, better put something on that eye," he says.

"It's okay," I say.

"Describe the guys, kind of car," he says, flipping open his black pad.

I describe what I can, can't remember what kind of car. At least three guys wearing suits, dark hair . . . .

"Dark hair," he says, lifting his eyebrows, snapping closed the pad and looking at me like if I'm not the same as the guys who snatched Scorpio I should be locked up for stupidity, having a black eye on the street at three a.m., wasting cop time on hopeless chases.

Though it's a warm night I find I'm shaking through the body.

"So you're walking down the street and out of nowhere these guys jump you and grab your friend, that it?"

"That's it," I say.

"No reason for this action."

"Look, I don't know."

It's getting later and later.

Where would they be now? Where would I go if were them?

"Couldn't we, like, drive around?" I say.

"Drive where? Which direction? You wanna tell us where to drive?"

"I'm just scared for my friend."

The words are pathetic; I want to go all the way and break out into a good open cry.

The cop puts his hand on my shoulder.

"Look kid, what's your friend's name?"

"Scorpio."

"Scorpio. That all. Scorpio what? Mr. Scorpio?"

"Scorpio. That's all I know."

"Know where this Scorpio lives?"

"No."

"No address. This Scorpio . . . he . . . ."

Then he softens.

116

"Look, I'll get on the radio, check around. You got a number I can reach you at in case we got to get in touch with you?"

"No," I say. "No numbers."

"No numbers," the cop repeats, looks at me, exhales. He's got an extra gun stuck in his pants and a rectangular pin on his chest says *In Memory of Morton Dillwener*.

"You look like a smart kid," he says. "Why you messed up in stuff like this?"

"I don't know," I say.

"You got some place to go to now? You okay?"

"Yeah."

"Okay, let us give you a lift home, kid."

When they drop me on my block I stop and lean my forehead against a phone booth feeling sick and helpless. Again and again I see myself hurtling into the car and then rising dizzy and moving and something solid hitting my face. I study the pieces of memory but can't find any right moves I missed, any way I could have acted different, changed what happened.

Then I think Scorpio must have known those guys and known he was in trouble. He wasn't surprised enough. I can't put it together. I realize I know nothing about him, the kind of life a guy like that lives, where he would live, what he might do when he's not shooting pool, where the clothes and the money come from. The open hours come back, his non-schedule, always the clean hair style and the well-kept look. And I feel something like rage; it's not rage itself but not altogether other than rage.

I touch my hand to my eye, which feels like mush, half-closed, pulsing, but surprisingly not bleeding. It feels like there should be blood. I sit down, back to the phone booth, listening to the yellow streetlights humming overhead and consider just curling up in the street until morning.

# 16

# Sour Grapes

*T*here's always a sting when I see the light on in the kitchen window when I get home late, a sick pang worse than fear, a sharpness of sensibility mixing guilt, irritation and resentment that I have to be confronted, humiliated after a long night when I've had emotional ups and downs of my own, when the short walk home in the air fresh after the smoke of the pool room is long, scraps of newspaper whirling along the avenue in chest-high eddies, bag ladies mixing the drops from cases of discarded liquor bottles into the Longest Island Tea of all time, whores my age cruising the streets sucking lollipops.

*Going out?*

*No.*

*Take me with you, please. I'll cook for you.*

*No thanks.*

*I'll clean for you.*

*I'm broke.*

*Take me home.*

Out of habit I ease the door shut with a faint click of the lock and move quietly up the stairs with a low quick step to minimize the creaking. There's always hope that Mom left the lights on to discourage thieves.

But no, when my eyes adjust to the light I see Dad sitting at the dinner table in just a white T-shirt and underwear eating from a large bowl of pink grapes.

"It's four-thirty."

"I know," I say, sitting down and unbuttoning my shirt, relieved and scared, tears in my eyes.

"What happened . . . You okay?"

It comes to me that he might be as angry as I've ever seen him, deadly quiet angry, fighting an explosion.

"I'm all right," I say.

"You don't look all right . . . Put some ice on that."

I go to the freezer and crack open a tray. When we spend afternoons watching football games there's a specialness about pouring lemonade on a glass of ice and letting it cool, eating crystal-salted pretzels to create thirst and sipping slowly to slake it.

"Want some ice water?" I ask.

"No I don't want any ice water, Christ what is going on with you. What is going on?"

I put half the ice in a face cloth and press it against my eye, fix a glass of ice water with the rest.

"Press the ice hard to it."

"Okay, Dad."

"Press it until it hurts and it'll spread the pressure around."

There's got to be an army story behind this somewhere—an old French boxer pushing a coin to his eye after a bar fight, but I won't get it tonight.

Dad's popping grapes angrily into his mouth with an occasional hard stare, spitting the seeds into the garbage can.

"I can't live like this," he says. "I won't live this way. You're messing up the whole house."

"I'm sorry, Dad."

"There are kids growing up in this house; your mother's working her tail off on that Campbell's spread. We want to come home to a decent sensible house. We can't have this."

"I know, Dad. I'm sorry."

"Sorry isn't good enough. When you live in your own house you can do whatever the hell you want. Waste your life however you want. But not in this house."

"All right, Dad, I'll be out soon."

"Nobody wants you out, but you're driving everyone crazy."

"Nobody needs to go crazy, I just. . . ."

"We can't sleep if you're running around all night in that pool room with those guys, maybe getting your throat cut, coming in at all hours all the time. Can't you see that?"

"It's not all the time. . . ."

"It's a lot of the time; it's too much of the time."

"Next year I'll be in college and. . . ."

"To hell with college, don't do us any favors, those colleges cost a godamned lot of money."

"I know they do."

"Don't go because you think I want you to."

"Don't you want me to?"

"Of course I do, but not if you're just going to screw around."

"I'm not just going to screw around. Can I have some of those grapes?"

Dad nods at them but doesn't push the bowl. We sit in silence; I reach for a grape to break the line across the table and realize I haven't eaten a thing since lunch break at school, that I'm starved. I snap off a cluster of grapes and scarf a few. One rolls off the table and I pick it off the floor and pop it in my mouth.

"Nobody wants you out," Dad says. "But I can't live like this. I'm not putting up with any more of this crap."

"Are you throwing me out."

"I will if you can't play it straight."

"What does that mean?"

"I'll tell you what it means."

They've got Scorpio in the car and are driving him around somewhere. What did he do to them? Could they grab him for no reason? It's not conceivable that he's really a bad guy. I can't think of him as actively immoral. Maybe a bad drug swap? Borrowing a payment to buy bananas for someone's sick mother? And he's out there alone while I'm here getting sermoned toward tears in the kitchen of a brownstone and saying "Okay, okay, I'll play it straight, Dad."

"You'll be home for dinner every night and you'll help out around the house, and if you go out you'll be back at a reasonable hour. That's not much but you'll do it or find some place else."

"Okay."

"Nobody makes big demands on you around here."

I can hardly listen to this, and pop one grape after another, a collection of seeds forming on the table.

"It's time to cut back. You're too involved in it all. It's all out of control. It's taking over and doesn't lead anywhere. You think you're in control but you're not."

"Okay, Dad."

"Don't okay Dad me, it will ruin your life."

"It won't. It hasn't."

"I'm telling you it will, take a look at yourself. Look at those rings under your eyes. There's purple under your eyes. Are you taking drugs? You can't sit still in a chair for one minute."

"I'm not on drugs, Dad. I got hit in the eye."

"Not both eyes."

His voice is throaty so he's not quite at the end of his rope. There's still a little rope left if I don't use it to hang myself by saying something stupid.

"It's a waste of time, Andy," he says, softer. "It's the time, not just playing, but the time thinking about it, not building for anything. I don't have anything against the game."

I reach for the bowl of grapes. I'd like to eat them all without stopping.

"Leave a few of those, okay."

I snap off another branch and slide him the bowl and he gets up and puts it in the refrigerator, closes it quietly. If only he'd slammed the thing.

"Clean yourself up and get some rest," Dad says,

the disappointment in his eyes much worse than the anger. "Andy, you need to have that thing looked at in the morning."

I wait until I hear the door of his bedroom close, letting the ice melt my eye numb.

"Whaas up, Andy? You win?" George says, rolling over in bed when I slip into the room.

"Nothing," I say. "See you in the morning."

"How much . . . You okay?"

"Yeah, I'm okay, get some sleep."

He snores lightly in a minute, a leg thrown over the edge of the bed.

In bed I can't sleep.

I lie in all my clothes with my heart pounding.

Outside the rain starts slowly. First drops, like someone's fooling with a syringe above. Then a lull and it blows in, that suddenly increased force and hard beating down, so emphatic that drops striking the window can't be distinguished.

When I close my eyes I imagine those guys in suits working over Scorpio. I still can't see their faces but those are the kinds of guys, I think, who string people to fences with chicken wire and cut off fingers for notions of honor and revenge. And in some way those are the guys Scorpio hung with, his people.

I see him tied to a chair in a warehouse by the river. His feet disappear to the knees in a plastic wastepaper basket. He's out cold but starts coming to when they dump in the first shovelful of cement. The stuff hugs his feet; he can't move. Maybe he tries to cut a deal, appeals to old times, tells them what he'll do for them if they give him a break, but stops himself, realizes he isn't holding any cards. And if he speaks they don't answer him but just put in another shovelful of cement. And he knows then he's going into the Hudson with the eels. And he tries not to think what it will be like in the river. And probably he does not think about whatever he did to get there or pray for someone to bust in and save him or think he can escape like he's so often escaped traps on the pool table. A knot grows; the heaviness of the cement spreads. And as the cement clings around his knees and one man puts away the shovels the terror spreads from his heart in burning streams along his eardrums, through his throat until he couldn't scream if he wanted to, even if he thought it would do him some good.

I have been dozing and now find myself frozen in my bed in terror. The grey light comes in and I know I'm emerging from a nightmare but cannot remember what it is. I've never remembered a dream but can often feel that the dreams have been good or bad. Now there's nothing in my head but a fear so strong it prevents me from moving, pure concentrated fear. I strain to move and can just make out the sweat sopping my shirt like blood in the glow of the streetlights. I hear steps outside my body by the windows and in the hallways and know I'm both in some unawake state and out of it, being forced to lie still while the linoleum click of shoes closes in on me, lying intensely alert but paralyzed, and I lie back making a desperate effort to break the bind or cry out, knowing that if I can move so much as a finger or call out to somebody out of the dream it will all be over and I'll be back in the world; I lie struggling without muscles, unable to connect mental signal to muscle, and when I finally move the casing springs from around me and there's just the warm morning air and damp sheets, my heavy breathing, a car noise coming from the streets.

# 17

# Graduating

*H*olidays, birthdays, special occasions have never meant anything to me, and like most people who don't like them or find them time for celebration I suspect all those happy types who do of being fakes or stupid. April Fool's Day's the only holiday that seems a good idea.

The whole family comes to graduation, including my Connecticut grandmother, the ketchup thief.

We seniors sit on the stage capped and gowned in assembly for the last time, one by one walking to the podium and applause. Some of the girls are tearful as they return with their diplomas. They're such nice people I feel out of place being on the same stage. When the principal hands me mine he can't help a politic grin at my black eye, now at its deepest violet, a grin that says to the students *I was once a kid too* and winks to the parents *but it is still good to have this case gone*.

That night there's a big party at the house of a rich girl on Riverside Drive. There's dancing in three different rooms and I stand around with some of the guys mixing tequilla, O. J. and grenadine, watching the bright half of the rainbow rise in glass pitchers. Remarkable every time. A bong's travelling the room and I hit on it, the smoke burning my lungs. Unavoidably, we tell borderline sentimental stories of freaks and fights: Dalton's center Link, who proved incontrovertably the theory of evolution, a maniac who pulled the endpost out during a soccer game and threw it at the referee as if spear-hunting zebra, the time we almost had a gang fight outside a church gym and this guy pulled a wooden rolling pin from under his leather jacket, as if his parents had padlocked all the silverware at home and that was the only weapon he could find. We'd argued on the court and they were waiting. None of us wanted to fight, but didn't want to back down in front of each other, and it looked like the fight might happen. But when that guy pulled the rolling pin it was tough not to laugh. I look at Jonesy and Mike and think of bringing the ball up to center court and passing to Jonesy and getting it back and swinging it to Mike behind an Al screen for the jumper he never missed much.

Betsy's making out in the corner with Wilson and a few minutes later I see her slow-dancing with Al, and then I don't see her until she's standing in front of me, visibly tipsy but coherent.

"Andy," she says. "Will you come out on the terrace with me."

"Whooooooaaaaa . . ." some of the guys say, and I give them the smirk they expect and, wordlessly, follow Betsy onto the terrace, half-wondering whether I'm on her make-out list, since surely I've earned it with patience since fifth grade.

Betsy's wearing a blue dress with a belt and has filled out into a Real Woman with a broad straight back and big soft breasts and wide hips. Not a traffic stopper, even plain, but my heart catches a little. In a few years she will be through her wild phase, never that wild, so far as I know, and settling down in some kind-hearted kid-care-related profession.

"I wanted you to do something for me," she says, and I suspect in her tone that she's known all along that I've liked her—sensed it the way people always can when someone they don't like-that-way likes them that way—not wanted to show that she knew I'd been able to fool everyone but her. And I guess she's sorry she's held my card so long without playing it.

Or maybe she never had a clue.

"The time goes fast, doesn't it?" she says, wistfully. "Do you remember when we were in fifth grade?"

"Yes," I say. "I do."

"Remember holding hands in the playground, pushing each other on the swings."

String section, fortissimo.

Betsy, will you waltz this last waltz with me?

But for a moment I do see the little girl in pony tail chasing after me and laughing, barked knees and bandaids, legs bending like rubber as she springs up from a fall.

"Well, I just wanted to say that even though we haven't been the closest friends in high school, I've always considered there was something special between us, a kind of bond. You have a good soul, and I'm going to miss you very much."

"Thanks," I say, wincing at "bond" and then "soul," "I'll miss you too."

But when we converge in a hug I feel the scene artificial, almost distasteful, like it's pointless and soggy hugging on the porch at a last party when nothing matters anymore, riskless as nine ball for nothing, and playing nine ball for fun isn't fun, though I can't help but feel her bust against me, and the attraction's still there.

"Sign my yearbook, Andy," she says, tipsily. "Sign on your page. And I'll sign yours."

"I forgot mine," I say, opening to the full page picture of me with a corny meditative gaze seated on a rock in my favorite navy turtleneck sweater at the edge of Sheep's Meadow. If she signed mine she'd elaborate about my good soul and our bond and move on to "soul-bonding" or say how sorry she was that in second grade she beat me in an arm-wrestle—she could probably still cream me in an arm-wrestle. Everyone chooses a quotation to put under their photo, something from a record album, one of Murphy's laws, *things will get worse before they get better,* or something literary no one's read. Mine's Edward Dahlberg, whom I've never read, having found the quotation pencilled on a buried index card/bookmark in the library. *A man who has not been decoyed is shrewd, which is icy insanity.* It's okay. I think I know what he means.

"Are you going to read what I write before you leave?" I say.

"Not if you don't want me to," she says.

"I don't."

I seat myself on the terrace wall and gulp from my pitcher of Tequilla Sunrise for inspiration until the inspiration numbs my brain enough and I start. *Dear Betsy, I'm not a licensed physician or a believer in last days of judgment so I shouldn't give advice, but I still advise against marrying anyone who calls waterskiing H-2-0 ski-ing, actually, anyone who waterskis at all. I also recom-mend against men whose first names should be last names, like Smithson or Sherman.* But I can't get much going. It's all mush or evasion of feeling behind word gre-nadine. I make my hand keep moving over my pic-ture until I've completely effaced myself, and pause finally to consider how to sign off. *Your friend* or *your dachshund* or *feelingly?* Tequilafully yours, Andy, I write, and when I close the book and hand it back to her I see she's been staring at me with such a soft moist look of good feeling that I think, ah yes, this is the way I must remember her, as one intimate fantasy never cured.

# 18

# Stick Ups

*T*here is not much better in life than good food late at night when you're drunk.

I slip out of the party for a few quick goodbyes and head up Broadway for Mike's Pizza Joint, buzzed and tired, happily possessed of enough cash to buy a meat ball sandwich with extra cheese and a cold Diet Pepsi in a can. The cheese sticks to the roof of my mouth and the sauce is rich and hot with dried peppers. Outside a wino couple goes by kissing sloppily, her arm up the sleeve of his coat, the two almost falling down, me catching a glimpse of pink tongues out too far and rising, walking out in the opposite direction from them, thinking, *But who am I to talk about technique,* who am I, alone, stumbling out of a pizza shop, not waltzing away graduation night, instead holding off my aloneness for inspection, remote and beside me, finding the theatre of this and life in general actually nice as I quicken, as if drawn, until I'm there and climb the stairs and round the corner and walk around to the back, shake hands with Andre and

Sammy the Gin Player in his high seat facing the player table.

*Hey kid, hey kid.*

*Dice be nice, who wants some.*

*Ten's the point.*

*Ah-ten-shun. Tension.*

*Twenty open, how much you want, kid?*

"Not now," I say. "Not now."

On the player table Andre the Great's practicing, performing between the acts of bigger games. Andre loves to take two balls from a full rack and shine them ceremoniously and set them in some crazy frozen rail position for a seven-rail bank shot, to clean the table and brush the chalk around the tip of his cue for twenty minutes like he's oblivious to the balls on the table, to everyone else, like he's a poolosopher. He runs his hands over the waxy waves of his hair, working his face into all sorts of expressions. Then he shoots the shot maybe seventy times, slowly, deliberating over it, his forehead wrinkled with concern, never making a ball. He talks to the balls under his breath and calculates in the air and brushes the table more so specks of dust won't block his pool lines and all the time he doesn't make eye contact with anyone, though there are ten tables empty in the back and he's playing in front of twenty people. The shots can be made.

So what?

What's the use?

When he makes his shot once every six months there's a cheer for "Andre the Great, Andre the Great," and that's his moment, and Andre smiles humbly as though he hasn't known anyone was watching him and is embarrassed to be caught in a public display of such mastery.

I sit against the back wall and the tequila moves to my limbs leaving my mind suddenly clear and sharp and I look out over the table at Andre, nodding to myself, realizing in successive nods that I will never be a great player, that it isn't in me, and that I will not spend my life playing pool, practicing shots, that I couldn't if I wanted to, that yes I'll go to college and win a campus trophy and get nicknamed "jaws" and hustle a little in redneck bars with neon bar signs in towns where to be in is to be out, where they call Burger King the B. K. Lounge and cruise for chicks. I'll walk into places where having to wait if you lose is worse than any money involved and know the thrill, the tropical overgrowth of possibility, bent cue sticks and chipped tips and dead cushions, and know flat out that I can take anyone in the place, but that it isn't worth much, and will be worth less and less, and will end someplace, and that's okay.

So is Dad right in saying the real issue's time?

It's a beautiful game, Andy, but it doesn't lead anywhere, doesn't build?

Once an artist, twice a pervert, and the time going, going, slipping away . . . gone playing it, thinking it, and the essence of good gambling's knowing when to quit?

I train my eye on the door expecting each moment to see Scorpio come bouncing in with his Hawaiian shirt all full of painted birds and hair all slick, eyes taking in the corner of the room, chewing air.

Maybe he's just dropped out of sight for awhile?

I close my eyes and see him being chased by lean hit men in dark glasses and suddenly the hit men turn into beautiful tanned over-breasted women on some tropical island, catching up to him through the surf and then in backless gowns rubbing his shoulders in the casino, Scorpio pushing in his chips, then scratching the green felt of the black jack table for another card.

Maybe Scorpio was thrown in the river with cement shoes and his bones have washed halfway to Puerto Rico.

An example?

Well okay.

But if so, for whom?

For the underworld: Warning, do not piss on Mobster X's cape or Gangster Y's.

p.s. We mean business.

An example for me in some larger way, another angle in the plot of the universe to make me *play it straight* unless I go on saying "When it doesn't matter there's no pressure" until there's no pressure so that it must not matter? And what anyway is this sense that the universe is always in conspiracy to keep us from what we love?

I look around the pool room.

Killer's playing eight ball with a poke-and-hope calibre traveling salesman who snaps his fingers and points at the pocket on every shot, curses his "shape" when he leaves himself long, calls the low balls "smalls." The man doesn't have any concept when he lowers and it stings my eyes to watch him. Killer breaks and the cue ball flies off the table and he stumbles off after it. "Don't hit it so hard, Killer-Diller," Freddie yells after him. "Just cause the ball's white don't mean you got to kill it." Rebel's asleep against the cue-rack with an uncut cantaloupe in his lap, one hand resting on the canteloupe as on a baby doll. Suddenly I want fresh air and a breeze and walk down the stairs and out toward the river.

Along the avenue and close up against the stone of the buildings the grate people sleep in tattered over-coats over hot air vents, torn cardboard boxes laid over them for blankets. I walk through the stone aqueducts that tunnel beneath the West Side Highway, the path winding steeply down past a tight-curved cinder track that looks from above like a neat dark string, leading past a playground with swings to the bannistered river walk, to a pier and marina where there are always eel fishermen, sometimes barbequing eels over trash-can fires and drinking Buds.

On a bench by the marina, beneath a flowering oak, Sweat Drops sits with his head resting in his hands an elbow's length above his knees, and doesn't look up until a moment after I sit down beside him.

"Hey kid," he says. "How you doing, kid?"

"Not so bad, Sweats," I say.

"Have a drink, kid," Sweats says, handing me a whiskey bottle, from which I swig deeply.

"Hey," he says. "A kid like you shouldn't be down here drinking whiskey like that."

"I like being down here," I say. "It's what the doctor would have ordered."

"Don't worry about it, kid," he says, smiling so I can see his brown rotted teeth. "Even I can't get pussy every night."

"I'm not worried about it, Sweats," I say.

We sit watching the outline of Jersey grow into dark relief, the sky greying slightly against the black of the land.

"Kid," Sweats asks. "You ever feel like killing yourself?"

"Nah, Sweats. Don't make no sense. Give me another shot of that whiskey."

"Sometimes I feel like killing myself," he says, and gazes off at the West Side Highway.

"You a manic depressive or something, Sweats?" I say.

"No, I ain't no manic depressive. I'm a manic aggressive," he says.

Cars zoom by on the highway.

Not far from here we played craps under the aqueducts, Sweats, myself, about seven others, and a wino came out of the bushes with a gun and told everyone to back away from the money.

I see about a hundred bucks on the ground and us all looking at it and then at the gun glinting in the man's hand and the man's swimming eyes and I see us all stepping back but Sweats, who puts his hand under his bag-mannish coat and comes at the wino saying "Make your play, sucker, make your last play, sucker," until the man hesitates, confused, then goes tearing off yelling strings of curses about how every white man in America thinks he's Clint Eastwood.

"You gotta gun?" Freddie says, incredulous.

138

"No," Sweats says, and holds out both hands with an enormous grin.

"You're a sick fucker," Rebel says. "You need psychiatric fucking help."

Sweats looks at the money, still scattered on the ground, and it dawns on him that what he's done is worth at least three bucks a man.

"That's right," Jersey Red says. "Stick us up now, park ain't safe now for nobody."

"Careful or he will," Freddie says.

"Police ain't never around when you needs them," Jersey says.

There's an argument about whether to pay him.

"Hell no I ain't paying," Jersey says. "No way. Want to give my money away give it to the man's really got a gun. You give him three dollars and wait in the bushes with your pants down."

"Pay the man," says Phil-up the Pot, a fat poker player always running late for an appointment with the Mayor of Atlantic City.

Gonzalez stares on blankly, only a slight smile on his face.

"You stay out of this, Gonzalez," Freddie says. "You talk all the time. I'm warning you, motormouth. I've had enough of this. You give me an earache."

Panama takes a silver dollar from his hat and says "Heads we pay him tails we don't" and starts to flip before Freddie snatches the coin and tells him to put the thing away, "Fathead."

"Eh eh eh three dollar," Killer mumbles.

And it's clear the game's gonna be held up until

139

Sweats has been paid and there's no point fighting over a lousy three bucks.

Sweats collects with disdain like we're all a bunch of petty thieves and it's degrading to handle our filthy money and immediately he starts throwing the money after every number as if he can't wait to get rid of it.

In ten minutes he's down to his last dollar.

"Can't never get a fucking break," he keeps saying. "Never a lousy-stinking-god-damned break."

"You ain't lying," Jersey says, scooping up a fistful of singles with a little hop.

"That's the plain honest truth, you ain't got no luck at all."

"No luck at all," everyone echoes.

Sweats starts walking off into the bushes.

"Come on," Freddie says, puts his arm around him and starts steering him back onto the lamplit pavement. "I got to take you back to prison."

"Fuck off, Fish," Sweats says. "I'm warning you."

"Back to Sing-Sing," Freddie says. "Sick leave's over."

Now on the bench near the river there's a salt breeze and a sliver of pink and silver that brightens the swells of grey green water on the Jersey side. The skeletons of half-constructed condominiums and rigid cranes rise out into hard relief. Sweats looks at me like he's waiting to hear one single reason why he shouldn't put stones in his coat and jump the token impediment of the rail by the river. The deep dirt-black wrinkles in his forehead are like cracks in pavement.

"Sweats," I say. "Don't kill yourself, I got a better idea."

"What better idea?"

"Listen up. You go into the fanciest restaurant around, right."

"Right, kid," he says.

"You order champagne, escargo  . ."

"What's that?"

"Snails."

"I don't want no fucking snails. A gun's easier."

"Listen to me, Sweats. You order yourself a fat juicy steak, most expensive dessert on the menu, chocolate fucking cake with raspberry sauce. Sip a few brandies. Then tell the waiter to kiss your ass."

Sweats thinks over my play for about a minute, then frowns deeply, shakes his head.

"No kid, wouldn't work," he says.

"Why not?"

"They wouldn't let me in the fucking restaurant."

"I don't know."

"Look at me, kid."

"But don't kill yourself yet. I'm gonna think of something."

"Yeah. Thanks kid, I mean, what do you get out of it?"

"No sweat Sweats."

# 19

# The Heifitz of Busboys

*T*he Holiday Bar and Grill's much the same; the cooks haven't learned any more English in the last nine months, but still manage to communicate an endless stream of profanity through gesture. They've still got the same four raunchy jokes each, told at every opportunity. "Ernesto, you're sick," I say, and if I slip him a few rum and cokes he fixes me steak au poire. Every one of the cooks signals after every waitress that he's the only way she will ever know the extent to which paradise is available on earth. "One kiss, one kiss, Kelly. One kiss. You like very much where I kiss you."

In a week or so I'm back into the routine, bringing water and coffee and clearing dishes, wiping out ashtrays and bringing fresh napkins and wiping down the laminated tables, bussing back the heavy plastic bins where the waitresses pile dirty dishes. I mop the bathrooms, trim dried philodendron leaves, towel mayonnaise spots from the velvet sleeves of debonaire octogenarians. There's a neatness, rightness to it all, tables turning and turning again and all those turning them getting paid. The rush hour, the calm, following orders. Good physical work, the kitchen hot enough to be a health spa if there was a masseuse. We rush about slicing bread and placing it in baskets below the ovens, covered with a moist checkered cloth. Trucks pull up in front of the white bannisters of the outdoor cafe and the customers sit in the shade of striped umbrellas watching us unload crate upon crate like stevedores.

Sometimes I have visions of a busboy who has chucked everything aside to become the Definitive Busboy, the Heifitz, and who works himself to where he feels the pulse of the dishes beat against the stone of his palm, feels in the cups clasped beneath the china of the dishes the possibility of an appalling freedom.

This Heifitz of Busboys would live alone in an ex-artist's loft stinking of turpentine near the restaurant. He'd borrow his own set of dishes, one of everything from the restaurant and a restaurant table, wine glasses, carafes and bread plates, and practice moves, arranging the dishes on his arm, out long and curving like a violinist's. "Your check's a deposit," the manager would say, eyeing him intently. "These dishes are a deposit," he'd say. They'd leave him alone after awhile. He'd have refused promotion several times and insist on double shifts, on working a two-man station by himself. He'd practice on his days off, not sleep until he'd gotten some problem solved, some move right, go over and again over the settings and resettings of tables, remembering the positions of the dishes for hundreds of turnings the way a chess player holds the history of past games in his head looking for breaks and new approaches beyond the known lines, variations. He'd learn ways of putting dishes down so that eaters felt the food appearing before them as though their imaginations conjured it, so it seemed desire itself had materialized the food. He'd find ways of pouring wine so that the wine seemed to well up like spring water from an unseen fountainhead at the bottom of the glass rather than being spilled from above. And then at the end there'd be mastery, gliding around the floor as if on skates, knowing the floor the way a blind man knows the furniture of his apartment, twisting between tables and hanging spider plants, his presence unfelt, causing dishes to leap into his hands and arrange themselves, mastery.

The Heifitz is just performing the coup-de-grâce on the table of your hypothetical blonde alligator-shirted yuppie couple when a woman with half her face sagging and shapeless sits down in plain sight of the bar. It's a busy moonless night and the cooks have turned off the salsa music and work in steamy silence. The water-balloonish half of the woman's face is blotched purple and pink like a tropical fish's, her breath a wheezing, a whistling like a boy with a stuffed nose snoring. Aware that her presence is revolting to those around her, the woman eats quickly, though with difficulty. It's a little hard at first to understand how, because an odd discolored appurtenance of flopping skin hangs where a chin and her neck ought to be.

And a hush falls over the restaurant. The rat-tat-tat-tat of the salad man's knife from the kitchen dominates the faint throb of wordless disco beat that John the Bartender says he's figured out statistically most

145

increases thirst. The woman sits alone, dishes before her, the waiters drawing cut drink mixers to see who will bring her the dessert tray, and some of the busboys eating off the old customer plates in the hallway, mixing morsels of salmon, lobster, and brandied duck into strange concoctions within themselves, waiting for the woman to leave before bussing her table.

And suddenly I'm the Heifitz, measuring my steps, tightening the reins, slowly, deliberately. It's not my station but I move on her table. The woman fixes her good eye on me as I near, seeing only her plates, swabbed clean with the dark house bread, her ashtray spotted faintly with olive green pesto sauce, her empty wine glass, carafe, which I hook under her dishes.

"May I show you the French desserts?" I ask.

# 20

# Second Thoughts

*F*or three weeks I don't go near the pool room; I work a few double shifts and play basketball on nights that stay muggy after the yellow park lights have come on. The games are hard and the tiredness bone deep so there's sweetness afterwards to long steamy baths with a magazine. But slowly the desire to shoot pool builds again, the dull magnet recharges itself. It gets harder and harder to walk by the entrance without turning in; there's a sickening feeling when I pass, tired and hungry for action after a shift, my pockets crammed with the busboy roll, feeling the action draw, evenings passing and the action untapped, a sense of the waste of possibility, my blood cement.

And inevitably the desire to feel the slow rolls gets too strong, and I go up those sticky stairs once again and look at the tables and take out a set of balls, shoot like a stiff for an hour and am almost convinced that I don't need it anymore, and am back after work the next day for an hour and a half, and so on, an hour or so before dinner every day, until I'm in deadly afternoon stroke, always turning down games and practicing, wanting no oppositional contact, just the pool.

Around the house they still think I'm basically recovering, mending like the now faint bruise around my eye, and they don't notice when the small action starts, it being easy to account for stray hours when you hit certain checkpoints, and I get into a few good games and the powers start nibbling again, and the clock hands bear down. My game gets tauter than it's been before, cue ball control finer, leaner, my whole game more focused. I go deeper and deeper in, the afternoons shortening on me, pinching, the minute hand of the pool room clock whipping the hour hand like a jockey at the 7/8 pole rising and leaning into the home stretch, the fast hand beating the slow into a metallic gallop.

"Let's make a game, baby," Legs says, leaning against the powder rack, watching me practice, picking his teeth, the sky a grey glare above the buildings, pool room light mixed to consistency with the grey of the streets.

"Come on, young blood. Make a game."

I rifle a ball into the corner, slow roll one, feeling like I can't miss, the pockets inescapable funnels, stroke easy and sure, the cue ball freezing through the stations of a tight run. Pocket, draw. Pocket, slow follow, hard, soft, inching around until the table's clean.

"Okay," Legs says.

"Okay what?"

"We's here. Let's go. You and Legs."

148

"Spot me."

"A cuestick. Be a man now, baby."

His face creases with laughter.

I take a handful of balls from the return and scatter them over the table, my eyes still on Legs, who's head's stuck forward and wags around on his neck. I pocket a ball and the cue freezes dead motionless as if it's been where it is forever.

"Young blood, stop flirting. This ain't a school-yard. There ain't no see-saws in here. You see any see-saws, baby. I ain't got no funky pony tails. This is a pool room, baby."

It's late afternoon and I've promised Mom to be home for a family dinner with my Uncle Joe and Cousin Ron. We only see Joe once or twice a year since he's moved to California; my Connecticut Grandma comes down, usually with an envelope containing a Hallmark card containing no inscription but somewhere between three and five one dollar bills, so the meal has a Thanksgiving-Christmas dinner status and I ought to be there, just put the balls into the plastic carrying tray and walk out and make my little responsible good son contribution.

"Make a game," Legs says.

"Not today," I say, turning. "I gotta run."

"Tomorrow? You been running all your life, baby."

"I'm done running, Legs."

"Then make a game today, baby."

The balls spread before me. I pick up the cue and freestroke in a cut shot, motion absurdly easy, some-how empty, almost mechanical, cue ball racing around the table and right back to my stick, like a dog taught to heel. I look at the balls on the table and know I can run them dead out so easy the doing's almost a bore.

Smart money still says *Don't play Legs,* says *he's too tough at the table to control,* says *you'll have to shoot full strength to win and he might bust you even if you do. Anytime it really matters to him he can get his game stronger than yours, bring himself out on a higher level.*

But something pulls me to him, pulls his game level within range, whispers deep down, *You can take him. Play your game and he's yours.*

Smart money says *Wait for a tropical and set a win-lose time-limit for quarter to six and relieve the man of twenty or so dollars before dinner so later in the week he'll want to play again and you'll make him your pet tropical and keep him in a pocket aquarium where he'll never quite learn your game and always beat himself so you don't have to bring in too much line at once. You'll put him in your pocket and educate him slowly until, if he's a respectable tropical, he'll stop caring that he can't win, and go on making appointments.*

But these days I'm not much for this sort of thing. Against weak players, when a little butter spread evenly would ease out more cash, I win fast as possible. Hustling's a waste of talent, ugly and small, a waste of all that's fine in the game. If I'm going to play it should be against myself in the corner in dead afternoon before a shift or against players like Legs all night, until my cue arm aches up into the shoulder socket and the sun's slanting crazily through the great bay windows, knifing the walls—play all night feeling the action something restless and alive in my gut, away from those zones where the intensity gets lost and winning's only marginally preferable to losing. The only thrill's in precision or games that might turn into battles I can't predict, time zooming away, where I have to grow harder or get beat, the action electric and every slip costing some of my busboy roll, four settings, three water pourings, two ketchup marryings, until I'm scraping for change for one raisin bagel at the corner Bagel Bazaar and a *Daily News*. But always the sense, the voice: *If you're really on your game you never have to miss,* that *as long as you've got the cue ball it doesn't matter who's on the other side of the table.*

No law of averages says you ever have to lose.

*Take Legs, he's here at the table to be taken. Take Legs,* says my cue stick, levelling in front of the duck run. *Take Legs,* and plop-stop, the first one's gone, pocket, stroking through.

"Okay, Legs. Shoot you for an hour."

"An hour. Lord have mercy."

"I gotta split in an hour."

"Got to? Why you wanna run before we hit a ball, young blood? You don't shoot so bad for a white man, you can hold a stick. Why you so scary all the time?"

"I'm not scary."

"You's terrified. You's fixin to quit before you starts. What's your hurry, baby? Where you got to run to anyway?"

"Dinner."

"Dinner. You hungry? You gonna starve if you don't eat dinner? You want me to order you some

151

babyfood so you don't starve? You wanna shoot the Great Table Legs with a spoon in your hand, baby?"

"Okay, Legs."

"Okay what."

"Rack the balls for a fin."

"What?"

"A fiver. Rack em."

"Not me."

"Rack the balls."

"A funky five dollar?"

"You got something better?"

"Nothing better than you, baby."

"Then get your stick."

"Keep talking."

"I'm talking."

"Talk and pay."

"If I lose. Rack the balls, sucker."

"Flip for the hit."

"Call."

"Heads."

"My break, baby."

"So break."

And I break, leaving the cue ball long.

# 21

# First Hours

"So whadda you wanna do, young blood?" Table Legs says. "You wanna shoot pool or just stand there like the fool you is?"

I stare at him while I chalk my stick, go back to studying the position of the balls as if he's not worth answering, trying to find the key into the run. It's dark out. Colored lights glow from the traffic below.

"I'm shooting pool," I say. "When I miss you can shoot."

"Then shoot, chump."

"Quit if you don't like my speed."

"A man'd have to be a lunatic to quit an all-day-long sucker-fool like you."

"And you ain't a lunatic?"

"The kid," Freddie says. "You tell him, kid. Shoot strong on his ass, full speed ahead. Shoot strong."

Yeah, I tell myself, shoot strong. Concentrate on matters at hand. You missed the silly dinner. It wasn't the right and considerate long-term play but you made it and it'll go on the long-term report card and be paid for when pay-up time comes but now you're here. You made your play, go through with it.

But I can't help seeing them gathered, the table nicely cluttered with Grandma's good dishes, a shine to the silverware, seven-layer cake maraschino cherried on silver trays, Dad saying, "Maybe we should just start without him and he'll be around in a few minutes," and Joe's wife saying, "We can wait a few minutes, we're not in a hurry, are we Joey, honey?" and Grandma pointing out that I'm "a big boy now" and Mom thinking through her embarrassment and anger, *but that rat fink promised, he gave me his word.*

"Maybe he just went for a walk someplace for chrissake," Sarah will say while George, knowing better, picks at the crispy duck skin and the adults sip the Scotch Ron usually brings and makes talk more Chivas than Regal. Joe will start off on one of his cinema roundups, his taste in movies so astonishingly bad, so consistently opposite mine and Hank's that we've started using him as a reverse-litmus test: what he likes we're sure we won't; what he calls trash we rush out to see. Hank asks him deadpan, "So what's worth seeing these days, Joe, anything we shouldn't miss?" and Joe leans back, strokes his tie a few times and tucks it under his belt, finishes whatever he's chewing deliberately, then holds forth on contemporary cinema, Hank pursing his lips and working his eyebrows in mock-attentiveness—"Uh huh, yeah, uh huh"—nodding at each capsuled review.

Then there'll be a silence at the half-hour waiting mark, seven, and Dad, straightening in his chair, unable to keep the tightness out of his jaw, will ring the water pitcher with a fork, fold his hands on the table and lower his head for the grace:

"Rub a dub dub, thanks for the grub, dig in."

Dig in, I tell myself.

The nine-ball's dead on so positioning behind the thirteen will be a tricky bit of doing but it's the shot and if the first shot isn't right and hit with touch the whole procession of moves comes apart, becomes chance. English it upper right and stroke the object ball strong with rising left and the one will carry off the rail at a radical angle.

The ball only needs action.

So their meal will be strained. It will be strained if I'm there and strained if I'm not. Mom only tolerates Joe because he's Dad's younger brother, and she isn't crazy about Joe's wife, who always shows up in a dress that could double as a shower curtain, carrying a pound of some novelty shop food popular only with Hare Krishnas. Ron teaches high-school gym and without fail brings a new date each visit, some hardly older than I am, probably his students, like he can't just show up empty-handed, and I'm always embarrassed for the girl, who has to feel everyone's taxed politeness.

So their meal will be strained. Unfortunate, but not one of the great tragedies of human history, though it nags me to think of Dad at the head of the table, orchestrating the dinner, the flow of conversations not quite connecting, furious at me, anger like a restless physical thing in him, steaming in the back of his head.

And for a moment I think if I sprint home I can jazz

155

up some variation of the old triple overtime B-ball last game in Riverside Park excuse, something along the lines of it getting so dark no one could see the hoop, especially when the street lights blinked out. And though of course no one believes these to the letter anymore, the relatives will feel more comfortable, and Dad will appreciate my at least hustling back, working to make things go smoother. I'll bound the stairs in my sweat smell from the sprint home and wash the blue-black chalk crescent off before anyone sees it and come in saying something cheerful.

But there's still Legs across the table and the position of the balls, so sharp, the nine ball dead on and the rest of the sequence and other runs opening up and stretching behind, Legs looking at me now like I've been recaptured after an escape from Bellevue and he's working overtime to rehabilitate me into sense. There's still this night's worth of tight games, slow criss-crossing banks, the fact that I might take Legs tonight, and you don't quit good action in the middle.

I shake my head clear. I steady on the nine ball, straighten my bridge fingers, fan them out on the table and then bring them firm. I stroke the nine ball and it goes smack in and the cue ball snaps in a delayed reaction off the rail as if popping out of a stupor and continues around the table. Not perfect, precise. But enough behind the thirteen so I can position my way clear and run the balls out.

Legs lays his cue stick on the table and folds his arms, looking at me. He puts his hands on his hips and takes a deep breath. He starts to talk and then picks up the cue as if to unscrew it. The cue has green and orange decorations up by the joint, a strip of marble white at the base for balance. Custom made.

"Baby, you shoot like Godzilla himself for a funky five dollar," he says. "But I ain't got time for no five-dollar action, let's shoot pool, baby, let's shoot pool, baby."

"I'm shooting pool," I say.

"Five-dollar pool the hell you is. I don't do nothing for no five dollar. I don't drink ice-water for five dollars."

"What do you wanna play for, Legs?" I say.

"My grandmother don't roll for less than ten."

"Let's roll for ten then."

"The baby. Who wants some?" Legs says, waving a fistfull of cash. "Who likes the baby? Get down. Twenty open. Twenty's the point."

And we bet the tens, Legs sidebetting, then twenties, the loser breaking the balls, trading games until I've lost track of who's up, feeling only that I'm in it, that I can win it, that I can take him and be standing when we're done. The room fills with smoke, shadowy faces against the walls talking, dealing, betting our game, a haziness to everything but the balls vivid against the green under the hanging lights.

I bet extra on myself, bet with people I've never seen, different amounts with small bettors, holding the stakes in my top pocket. I make some good shots, starting to relax into the evening, put the dinner out of my head. That cake's crumbs now. After a dinner one only wants to eat again anyway. On the table: a cut shot, cue roll into position, then bang, stop with draw, bang, stop, and I'm collecting cash.

"Pay up, fools," I say, feeling high and loose. "Pay your dues."

"Shoot kyyd," Freddie says, pocketing bills.

It gets to be ten, then eleven. Two or three losses in a row can wipe me clean with all the side action but no one knows and that's bonus thrill, edge of sweet tension, an inducement to intensity, because backed down against my last dollar and sharp and feeling the pool juice coursing through my nerve endings I sense I can beat anyone, that my game's all razor, that no one could be sharper.

But Legs starts wearing me down. Talking, gesturing, staring at balls for minutes then shooting fast and neat, grinding at me with a mix of speeds.

"Okay baby, okay baby, okay baby," he chatters, moving around the table. "It's showtime, baby. Watch the cue ball. Pay attention now, baby. It's show time."

And I'm up, shooting his pace, banking balls home, "Rack-time, Legs. One for the good guys, Legs. Rack-time, rack boy," making those classy banks where the object ball circles the table and comes so close to kissing the still cue on its return trip to the hole that my spine shivers. Then he's back at me, like we're in a rhythm. I win a tight long game full of slow rolls, cue ball topspin sliding over the object, sending it back, and he wins one with a quick hard run. I start playing slower and trying to hold onto something, thinking out each shot, trying to control the tempo, thinking if I play slow like Old Sal and move and move he's got to let up—if I can defend like

158

Sal guarding the third-base line, snuffing every shot, he'll lose intensity, drop off. But I move too cautious and stiff a shot, hang a ball, and he licks his lips, smiles at me, nods his head—"that's my baby"—runs the balls out.

"When in doubt, run out, hey baby," he says. "Rack the balls, sucker. Rack em stack em, hey baby."

Sweat Drops, who's been betting hard money on me, mumbles out loud about how he's such a dumb-ass-sucker to be betting on a nut-case-dumb-ass-fucker like me.

"I got to see a psychiatrist bad," he says.

"Wouldn't do you no good, you fathead," Freddie says. "Shoot back on him, kid, shoot on him, kid. I'll put ten more on the kid. Ten open. Who wants some?"

# 22

# Three Handed

*L*egs is racking the balls and I'm powdering my hands and I look up and see Dad.

I turn and he's standing by a neighboring table. I don't know how long he's been there, watching, but his presence stabs me. Killer's trying to get him to play eight ball, one of his big hands resting on Dad's forearm. He's mumbling all sorts of things Dad could never understand. A star of David hangs over Killer's wide chest; the veins on his arms are like pipes on a wall.

I think for a minute Dad's going to hit me. I mean I don't know what to think. I'm startled, scared. It's a minute before I can breathe right. I think he's come up there to hit me and drag me out or curse me and tell me never to come near the house anymore, that I'm through and he's through playing father.

But he doesn't move. He stands there like he doesn't know what to do or what is supposed to happen, like maybe he's come to do or say something but has forgotten what he meant to say or changed his mind. He just looks at me and then at Killer Diller who keeps mumbling and then at me.

"Eh eh eh," Killer says. "Shoo some ayball, eh eh eh, dollar game ayball."

I have to say something.

So I say, "Dad, what are you doing here?"

The words stumble out but he hears me.

"Got restless," he says, "decided to take a walk."

"Up here?" I say.

"Why not?"

"Why the hell not?" Legs says. "You shoot pool too, daddy? You want in, we could play three-handed? You know. All three of us."

"You didn't have to . . . Dad," I say, stupidly. And then, "How's everything at home?"

He looks at me blankly.

"Are you kidding? Are you out of your mind?"

"How are the cousins? Grandma okay?"

"It's a zoo back home."

"I was just getting ready to leave," I say. "To go home."

"Sure you were," Dad says.

"You sure were," Legs says.

"Stay out of this, Legs," I say.

I have about forty-five bucks and won't have enough to pay the time if I lose. I figure there's no way I can let Dad see me get busted and pay Legs and the side action and then have to listen to Roger cursing me for stiffing the house. It's bad enough already, just seeing him here, the exhaustion in his face, his shoulders slumping halfway to the ground.

I lay my stick on the table.

162

"That's right, baby," Legs says. "Get with your daddy and get your funky freak ass out of here, go back to the zoo with the other animals and get your whooping like you deserves."

"Let's see you shoot," Dad says. "I don't get out of the house much in the evenings. Now I'm out."

"I can't, Dad," I say.

"Why not?" Dad says.

"Get on out with daddy, then," Legs says. "Get on home to your Grandma. We don't need no terrified scary ass zoo babies that doesn't want to be their own man in here."

"I just can't."

"Why not?" Legs says.

I take the rack off the balls and gather them and start placing them on the plastic rack. But Dad walks out from behind the other table and takes me by the arm. I mean he really grips right into my biceps. Seizes me with all the anger in his body.

He looks ridiculous in the smoky room with his loose tie and suit and polished leather shoes, ludicrous, a laughing-stock. He probably had the shoes shined in the subway before work.

"Don't whoop him here, now, Daddy," Legs says. "Have mercy, don't whoop him in a lousy no-good place like this, Lord have mercy, it'd break my heart to hear the baby cry."

"Can you beat this guy?" Dad asks.

"He doesn't mean anything with all that talk, Dad," I say. "He's just having his fun. He likes to talk. He's just mouthing off."

163

"I don't care what he means. I asked you whether you could beat the guy."

"Maybe I can beat him," I say.

"Hell no, you can't never whoop my ass. You neither Daddy. Never. No way."

Legs sits on the table between us and takes a ball off the rack and shines it on his black satin shirt, then sets the ball on the table. He takes another ball from the rack and starts shining it. His shirt catches and plays with the light.

"A no-shooting all-day-long scared sucker fool like you can't never beat a player like the Great Table Legs," he says.

"Right," I say.

"Damn straight," Legs says.

"I'd like to see what you've got," Dad says. "If you spend all your time here you ought at least to be able to shoot."

"I don't spend all my time here, Dad."

"You've spent the last two years here."

"Dad."

"It's the truth, Andy."

"I just don't want you to see me the way I am here," I say.

"The way you is," Legs says. "The way you is is you ain't got no heart at all."

He shakes his head and walks toward the cue rack to get his carrying case.

"Lord have mercy you's scary, scary when you gets up in the morning, scary at night. You shoots pretty straight when you ain't so scary but your heart ain't no bigger than a little green pea."

"Play him," Dad says.

"Come on, Dad."

"Play the man."

I say to myself: What the hell. Maybe losing in front of Dad's supposed to be the Grand Final Lesson in Real Life 101. I don't need this action but what the hell. Things can't get much worse.

I say to Legs: "Rack the balls, sucker."

Legs rubs his hands together and stands behind the table, licking his lips as he puts the balls on the table and places them one by one in the wood rack. Then he moves them back and forward along the table, all turning in sync, and lifts the rack delicately, talking at me.

"Baby don't wanna go home and get your whooping, well you doesn't have to, you can get your whooping right here if ya wants to. Come and get your whooping, baby. I'm gonna give it to ya."

"Take care behind when I break," I say, motioning him from behind the table with my stick.

I break too hard and Legs runs a few, then safes. I want to beat him quick, erase the scene, and move around the table with a fierce impatience.

"You young bloods acts like you's the ones running out of time," Legs says. "Got to cool your blood."

And he's right, but with Dad watching I can't shoot a lick. I'm tight, nerved out of my rhythm. I freeze when I lower as if my cue ball has stones in it like loaded dice, too conscious of every shot, of being clocked, a hitch in my stroke.

It's a mistake because I lose either way: a fool when I miss; a shark if I don't. I should have paid my time and left, cut my losses. It's bad enough without Dad having to see me get busted and have to listen to Legs.

And I lose without putting up much of a fight, my game sloppy, foolish, disgusting. I slip Legs the twenty and put the rest on the table and motion to the sidebetters that I'm tapped. They pocket the cash and move off. I sit down next to Dad on the bench near the powder rack and shrug, though my blood's still moving hard, pumping into my head. I toss my stick back and forth between my hands. My neck and throat burn with humiliation.

"What's that game you're playing?" Dad says. "I've never seen that game before. That some kind of a money game?"

"It's one-pocket," I say. "We each take a pocket and the first to make eight balls in his pocket wins. It's lots of defense. You have to keep the balls away from the other guy's pocket. You have to move them to your own pocket. Think ahead. It's a thinking game."

"Thinking game." Dad laughs.

"Anyway," I say. "I'm all through."

"I just got here."

"I'm broke," I say. "He busted me. Let's get out of here."

"That's all you're holding, you're broke already?" Legs says disgustedly. "Lord have mercy that's a shame."

"What were you playing for?" Dad asks.

"Twenties."

"Twenties?"

"Twenty dollars a game."

"That's a piece of money."

166

"I'm sorry, I know it is, let's go."

"Twenty dollars is a piece of money? I beg your pardon. You call that money. I mean, fuck you, sir," Legs says to Dad, strokes his shining wave of straightened hair, smooths it as if he's calming himself down, like he's ready to start swinging.

"Twenty god-damned stinking dollars. Now sir. Sir. I spend that much on cabfare every day. Twenty dollars. I don't walk nowhere. You come in here with a tie and shoes and a jacket and funky suit and call twenty dollars a piece of money? Do you know where you is? This is New York City, sir. This ain't no Turkey or Tennessee. This ain't no Mars. Where the fuck do you think you is at?"

"That's about enough," I say to Legs.

"I beg your pardon."

"Come on, Legs."

"Fuck you too, baby. You sorry scary ass no count baby."

The crap game in the back breaks up and Rebel, Sweat Drops, Gonzalez and Panama sit with Killer on the table next to ours. Killer looks from me to Legs to Dad with an expression between blankness and surprise.

"Shoo some ayball," he says to Dad, eyes wide, nodding his head. "Ayball," with a questioning shrug.

"No thanks," Dad says.

"Eh eh eh. Shoo some ayball?"

I'm still looking at Legs.

"What you gonna do, sucker?" Legs says to me. "Go cry to your daddy? You gonna cry, baby?"

And for a minute it's close. I have to fight the tears

back. They well up in my eyes; one starts squeezing out and I wipe it before it gets onto my cheek.

"Just ease up, Legs," I say, softer.

"Fuck ease up, twenty dollars. Ease up? You's a disgrace. I wipe my ass with a lousy twenty dollars. You want your lousy twenty dollars back. I wouldn't want you white folks to starve your funky assholes without twenty lousy dollars."

"Oh Legsy babe-bee," Panama says. "Make em see the light and the way to the truth."

Legs has drawn a roll of bills from his pouch pocket and he takes a twenty and crumples it and tosses it on the table, poking it around with his cue stick. Some more players from the crap game step into the light, eyeballing the twenty.

"Beat this guy," Dad says. "I'll put up the money. You shoot your one-pocket or whatever the hell you call it."

"It's not important, Dad, he's just running his mouth off."

"Do you shoot pool or don't you?"

"I shoot a little," I say.

"You shoot a very little," Legs says, breaking into an enormous grin that's almost crying laughter. "A very very very little. You shoot a very little when you ain't so scary. But you ain't got the slightest bit of heart. You got a heart half the size of a pea."

"Tell it to him, Legs, speak that truth to him," Panama says.

"Okay," Dad says, taking out his wallet.

Legs recoils in mock astonishment.

"You gonna shoot me yourself, sir, Daddy? You gonna pick up a stick against the great Table Legs?"

"No, he's shooting," Dad says, pointing to me. "I'm betting on him and paying if he loses."

"He's playing, you paying?" Legs asks. "That it?"

"Right," Dad says.

"Playing, paying. Goddamn. I beg your pardon. You paying?" Legs says.

Dad nods at him.

"Well goddamn. I'll play now, sir. But Daddy, Mr. Front Man, I won't play for no twenty dollars. Twenty dollars is an insult to decent folk. It's a disgrace. A bad shame. You wanna front against the great Table Legs you gonna have to show respect and you gonna have to come up with some money."

"Is fifty dollars a game all right?" Dad says.

"It will be all right for a start, Daddy," Table Legs says.

# 23

# Donuts with Rebel

$A$bout two weeks after the night watching Buddha I'm walking uptown from work and meet Rebel. He doesn't recognize me at first, asks me what the fuck I want. I say, "Rebel, man, don't you remember Seventy-ninth, Guys and Dolls?" and he looks closer, nodding at me as if no time's passed.

"Sure kid, just messing with you," he says. "Hey, how you been doing? See you gotta briefcase. You working?"

"Yeah."

"Tie and jacket. Man, you look clean."

"Okay, Rebel."

"Hey, I mean great, wow. Gotta job and everything."

"How about some coffee, Rebel?"

We sit down at the counter across from the grill man and when the waitress comes order jelly donuts and coffee. Rebel's cheeks are fat as ever, one with a long crescent knife scar I don't remember. I watch his chubby fingers drum along the formica counter, fingers which I do remember, doughy but firm around a closed bridge hand. His hairline has moved back a few inches and his forehead shines. He says he's feeling well and laughs about still getting welfare checks for his mental problems.

"I act like this in front of the doctor," he says. "Once a month."

And he starts doing mantras and chanting, opening and closing his arms like a sunflower until I can feel the stares of people in the booths behind us heating my back.

"And that jackoff says I'm making progress."

"Maybe you are making progress," I say, and order us another round of coffee and donuts while he tells me the latest, who's in jail and for how long, who still plays. Sammy the Gin Player died; Robby's in the hole for dealing smack—six years. Rebel says he doesn't shoot much anymore himself because the old pool room got made into a rug shop and at McGirr's downtown there isn't steady sucker action.

"It's a godamned hustler's convention down there," he says. "Bunch of crooks."

He mops his forehead with his T-shirt, exposing several rolls about his middle.

"Crooks," Rebel says, looks out the window, then starts fooling with his coffee cup, twirling around on his stool.

"I went up to the rug place the other day," I say.

"Makes me fucking sick," Rebel says.

"They ever catch Mousey the Thief?"

"No, that fucker's still at large. Hey, where you been shooting these days? I ain't seen you around anymore."

172

"I don't shoot much," I say. "I play a little chess sometimes at the Game Room, nothing much."

"Fucking chess," Rebel says, wiping jelly from his face, then licking his hand. "Game Room," he says, and looks at me, forehead crinkling with concern.

The grill man smooths out the grease from hamburgers he's just served and pours about half a cup of oil onto the grill and smooths it around. Then he unwraps a block of frozen hash brown potatoes and starts mashing it into the grease.

"That's some unfuckingbelievable shit," Rebel says, the donut frozen half way to his mouth.

"Saw Killer Diller the other day," I say.

"Yeah," Rebel says. "Where was that?"

"Up around Eightieth."

"Yeah, that sucker owes me money."

"Eh eh eh, he owes me money too."

"Son of a bitch, thought he was in Baltimore."

"Killer from Baltimore?"

"Son of a bitch owes you money too. Sucker owes everybody money, son of a bitch."

"He better pay me first," I say.

"Sure, he'll pay you kid."

"Ever hear anything about Scorpio?"

"Scorpio," he says.

"Bunch of guys jumped us one night. I kept expecting him to show again."

"Yeah."

"He ever turn up?"

"You were there the night they got him?"

"Yeah, but I thought maybe. . . ."

"No, they got him, kid."

173

And he puts down his donut and shakes his head until he's swallowed what's in his mouth.

"Too bad about Scorpio," Rebel says. "He was a good kid. Wasn't no fucking weasel like the rest of them."

"What happened to him?"

"You didn't hear?"

"Why do you think I'm asking you?"

"What are you married or something?"

"I was out of town for awhile. What happened to Scorpio?"

"Bought it, kid."

I lick the jelly off my paper plate, then fold the plate into a pizza-slice shape and put the point into my coffee cup. The hash browns are starting to sizzle on the grill and the grill man pours more oil on them and presses them until they're crusted brown.

"Holy shit," Rebel says.

"What'd they do to Scorpio?" I ask.

"Crushed him in a car pound, kid."

I push my coffee cup forward on the counter.

"Refill?" the waitress asks.

"No thanks."

"Coffee ain't that bad here, either," Rebel says.

"Why'd it happen? What'd he do?"

"Don't know what he did, kid. They don't need no reason."

And suddenly he looks like he's late for a train.

"Hey, gotta run," he says.

On the street I say goodbye, tell Rebel it was good running into him. My hand goes into my pocket like I'm reaching for my card, then I wave him off.

Already my ribs are pressing in.

"Watch that fucking chess, kid," Rebel says.

And he drifts down the avenue, looking in store windows like he's price shopping, poking around a pile of boxes outside a department store, finally out of sight.

Hilary answers the door to her place in flowered pajamas and puts her arm around me sleepily. I bury my face in her frizzy hair until she smells the liquor on me and holds my head off with both hands, asks me what's wrong with a look of such tenderness that I want to break into tears, and when we're in bed and I've pulled the covers over her I say, "Hilary, I'm fine. Go to sleep. I'm fine."

"Okay," she says. "If you're sure you're fine. But if you want to have a conference wake me up. We'll confer."

"I will," I say.

And when she's breathing rhythmically I look at her face, a faint pink flushing her cheek, and I marvel that after a day among those carnivore lawyers she sleeps so peacefully, so deeply, not a wrinkle on her face. Often when she's sleeping I watch her and her eyes open and catch me staring at her and she smiles.

"You don't ever ever ever sleep, do you?" she says in her cracked night whisper, and rolls over on her stomach and curls slightly and is asleep again.

I don't think I'll sleep tonight.

I ravel a strand of Hilary's reddish hair around my finger and adjust the blanket on her shoulders. Over breakfast I'll listen to her arguments and counter arguments about the case she's working on, and, if I can, express an opinion.

Now Scorpio hovers before me by the powder rack chewing a toothpick and chalking his stick in the smoky light kissing Laura in Riverside Park, the memories like stinging gnats that won't be shooed away. I see the two of them under the yellow streetlamp light, melded into one form, the bright redness of her dress and lips, the shadows of his cheeks, blackness of his hair, and I see his lifeless body dumped into a car trunk and the car being pounded by a wrecking ball and then crushed into one of those cubes that get varnished and sell for forty thousand on Madison Avenue.

What can I say?

It was a long time ago.

How long has he been dead now?

It is too late for mourning.

What can I say, Scorpio?

*I was one of you?*

*If there's a pool room upstairs, a Night Cafe where the old characters play craps on cardboard boxes against the walls at night, you'll be there?*

*Eyes fixed on the cue ball, stick smooth between the spread fingers of your bridge hand, bony and white against the green of the table, you'll be there.*

I've never talked with Hilary about the pool room, though I've wanted to. I'm not sure whether we're in love; I don't know what we are, but we talk about things; we'll sit in a restaurant drinking wine and talking, my hand tracing little circles on her thigh under the table, fooling with her hands when she removes mine to the table, whispering until the busboys clean ashtrays we're not using and take the candles off the tables.

Before I met her there'd been a string of nights alone, independence wearing thin in smoky bars amid suggestions that my destiny was solitude, so many nights thinking—drunk, my best thoughts are drunken ones—hot and flushed, taking the buzz to the edge of control, easing it back or pushing it delicately forward toward a finer edge, knowing already in moments of lucidity that the next day was being altered but dwelling instead on the astonishing sufficiency of cognac to the demands of the moment, the moment so much its own justification, the compensations it offered so real and worthy of whatever of the talents allotted I was squandering, as if there were such a thing as duty to one's talent, or such a thing as talent extractable from doing.

Now my life's getting mixed up in Hilary's, though sometimes she says she doesn't know me, says that I'm like a stranger, and I ask her what she wants to know, wishing it were easier just to find the wished-for words.

"Something you're hiding," she says.

"But I'm not hiding anything."

"Why is it that when they're not bragging men are so mysterious and quiet?"

"What's wrong with mystery?"

"It's not so warming."

"I'd tell you anything you wanted to know."

"Exactly."

"Make a questionnaire," I say. "Likes raw egg and wheat germ shakes? Likes aquatic sports, yes/no?"

About a week after I met her we were walking down Broadway and I saw Sweat Drops, who'd never been clean but now looked dirty way past caring. A street person. Terminally dirty. As we approached I wanted to take him immediately to Burger King and watch him scarf burgers and fries. I remembered so clearly drinking whiskey with him by the Hudson the night I graduated high school. When he passed I waved and our eyes crossed but he didn't seem to see me and I hesitated, but I didn't slow or call out. I wanted a flicker of recognition but he looked through and beyond me. Then I thought it'd been years since I'd seen Sweats and thought how much I'd changed physically since then, how Hilary laughed at my yearbook photo as a scrawny kid with hair parted absurdly to one side.

"Oh how cute you were," she said.

Probably Sweat Drops wouldn't recognize me in a stare fight. "Hey," I'd say. "Don't you remember the time we went to Atlantic City and I lent you twenty dollars?" *Sure kid, and you want twenty-five back.* "Don't you remember Robby showing Scorpio his dick and Scorpio calling it a fake? Don't you remember Robby and Nelson fighting in the street and dodging traffic while we stood in the window betting on the outcome, Jersey Red yelling wipe the floor with that sucker, hit that sucker, he's getting up again?" *Who won, kid?* "Don't you remember Chipmunk, Chipmunk the kid?" *Chipmunk. Yeah, how you been man? Hey, you got a ten spot I can hold til Thursday?*

In the spring light on Broadway I wanted to share Sweat Drops and the others with Hilary, to make her feel the old characters, their vividness. For a few minutes I was silent. But I could not see her in Burger King with me watching Sweats wolf burgers. I could not see her on the sticky staircase of the pool room, its odor rank with urine. That's not what she shipped for. The pool room would not admit her. She could come into the house, but not go up the stairs. Or rather, she could go up the stairs, but there'd be rugs there now. Sweats was farther and farther behind, rummaging through the corner garbage heaps.

"Andy," I hear. "What's wrong? You're covered with sweat and you smell like cognac."

"I do? I'm okay, really," I say, opening one eye and looking at her. "And I've got a plan."

"Are you sure it's not just a hangover? Does your plan include getting out of bed and taking a shower with me?"

"Don't you want to hear the rest of my plan?" I say, when we're in the shower.

"Soap my back," she says. "So what's your plan?"

"We could rent a car and drive . . . ."

"Andy, let go of me."

I realize I'm hugging her somewhat hard. Squeezing her, really. But I hang on for just a minute, running the cake of soap over her back.

"Andy, you're just a kook. Let go of me."

179

"It's a new form of massage," I say. "It's from the Ivory Coast."

But I'm still holding on. And my plan is this:

It's Friday. After work we can drive up into the Catskills and take a room in this motel we stayed at once above where the intersection of two rivers forms Junction Pool. There's a high metal bridge and the Junction Pool Motel's red neon sign on the right just off the bridge. Mostly it's a fisherman's spot. College was about half an hour away and spring of Senior year we'd drink on the wedge of bank between the waters and then pair up. Once I wound up with a girl named Suzie and told her about the time fishing with Dad and Hank when we saw the great gluttonous trout.

"Must have been a chub he ate," Suzie said. What a country girl. I was aroused.

"You got it," I said.

We had a six of Coors in the river keeping cold and when it got dark we stripped and waded into the water. Knee deep, we kissed, laughing at the lights of cars on the bridge. We kissed and I closed my eyes and pictured Gargantua the trout, grey-haired and moth-eaten now, licking his chops at the whiteness of my calves.

Hilary and I can sleep late in one of those beds that vibrates for a quarter and pack French bread and pâté and white wine and in the afternoon hike over the bridge into the Catskills. We'll make our way through the pine forests until we reach a clearing and when we get out into a good open field of low grass and wild flowers, patched with mountain laurel, we'll kneel.

"What in the hell are you doing?" she'll ask me.

180

"Come on," I'll say.

"Andy," she'll say. "You're giving me the creeps."

"Just kneel here with me."

And there, kneeling together, we'll have a conference and I'll tell her from the beginning about Scorpio.

# 24

# Chasing Legs

*I* stand by the large windows at the end of the pool room looking out over Broadway. On the corner of Seventy-ninth Street a man is unloading bales of newspapers from the *Daily News* truck while the driver of the truck drinks from a thermos. Night porters pile the day's waste from restaurants along the avenue in the streets. When I work the night shift at the Holiday we end by taking out the garbage, holding it out at arm's length so the busted bottles don't cut us through the plastic. When there are only three of us it takes half an hour and drips all over our clothes until we don't mind the smell.

It's cooler by the window.

I try to phase everything out that doesn't matter, everything except me and the shot to be made so that it's just me and the universe and the cue ball and the object ball. I try to get back to where it's me in a white room with nothing but a pool table and the cue ball and the object ball. The perfect table, well-weighted stick, no second chances, no prisoners, stroke soft and easy as apple butter.

I walk through the empty tables in the back of the large room to the bathroom and wash my face in the cold water and stand for a minute breathing heavily. The stalls stink and I breathe deep until I feel like vomiting and then spit in the urinal, flush, and exit to where Legs and a half-dozen men stand around the one lighted table. I don't look at Dad. I rack the balls for Legs back and forth, the balls rolling snug against the wood, press with the knuckles, lift the rack.

"Shoot, Legs," I say.

He shoots. It goes back and forth. I play well but Legs ups his speed and keeps his mouth shut and puts a little extra into each shot, the English finer, rolls slower, more deliberate. The balls get pushed back to the far end of the table and every shot has to be banked with the cue held safe so the games are long and tactical though we shoot fast and without interruption. I concentrate on the whole position of the table, thinking plays through, see the sequences played out. Legs picks his teeth between shots. He walks with his bounce step around the table, picking and chewing, then lowers. I win a game and he wins one and then we each win another. I get a black cherry soda and a cream soda for Dad who takes it wordlessly. I press my soda against my forehead and run the cold can over my cheeks. The clock above the soda machine slides past three.

"Let's make it two-hundred a game," Legs says. "Let's gamble."

I look at Dad and he nods at me. He pops his soda and takes a small sip and looks at Legs and me and nods again.

184

I nod back.

I can't wonder now whether he has two hundred in cash in his pocket or what he would be doing with two hundred if he did. He mostly pays his way with plastic, never holds much cash.

The game goes slower still.

I refuse to make any mistakes, safing or banking when I could take long straight shots I ordinarily try, picking off points when Legs misses. I beat him eight-to-three the first game and he pays. Dad holds the money tightly in his fist. I beat Legs the second game on a slow-rolling cut shot and he pays. I start feeling lighter, almost giddy like my game is coming compact, like I only have to be patient, keep on the concentration and not get happy and apply steady pressure and he will break before I do—the way it is when you get a guy's wrist in an arm-wrestle and control the strength flow until he cannot surge and wears himself down. It's like we're both underwater and I have more air left in my tank and all I have to do is wait for him to burst to the surface. And I am willing to wait. All night. All tomorrow. Until Christmas, since we're here, playing, shooting a tight, crisp game.

Legs starts taking chances. He tries tough combinations and I snipe off a few balls and safe him down to the end of the table. I pick off another two, safe up table. He makes a few great long cut shots but pays when he misses into an open table. We move into the end game. He banks and slow rolls the balls toward the pocket and I kick them away, kill the cue ball dead

185

stop with draw, leaving him long. I beat him a third game.

Dad's still got the money in his fist. I don't want to touch any money, nothing but my cue stick.

Legs goes into the bathroom for a few minutes. He likes to smoke a joint or blow some coke when he gets stuck and that's fine.

*Go junk yourself up, I think. Fill yourself with junk. Don't worry about me. It won't bother me if we wait three hours. It won't throw off my rhythm. When you come out all junked up I'm still going to beat you.*

*Pin your name on the back of your shirt, Legs, so they can identify the body. Cold Harbor, Legs.*

*I'm going to be sitting here waiting to ambush you and whoop you worse than you ever dreamed of being whooped.*

Legs comes out walking lighter. He's tucked his tight red pants up behind his high leather boots and walks with a bounce.

"You want something for the head?" he asks.

"No thanks," I say.

"Your daddy want any?"

"My father doesn't want any."

"You sure, baby."

"I'm sure."

"Okay, baby."

"Shoot, Legs."

I break again, pushing a few to my pocket and sending the cue ball long, but Legs gets control and I have to play straight defense for ten shots without any hope of turning it around. He makes several fabulous cut shots, turning the cue ball loose like you have to on such shots, trusting the position to the almost luck

186

of table sense, the gamble of feel. I bank a few home. He banks two. We safe back and forth. He slices another home.

Then there's just one ball left on the table.

Legs banks it for his pocket and it closes, then stops. I come behind with right-hand English and kick it loose and come back down to the safe end of the table. He banks it toward his pocket again, controlling the speed so that if he misses I won't have a return cross bank, trying to make the ball flatten into the rail, freeze to the lip of the pocket so that it is possible for me to bank the ball seven rails around the table for my hole or play it straight, knock the ball to the end of the table.

An Andre position, the kind that never happens in a game, but there's no time to marvel.

I walk to the powder rack and rub some of the fine powder between my bridge fingers, looking at the table and the two balls, one frozen a foot from the pocket, imagining Scorpio back from wherever he is, how he'd chew over the ball, and I lower, concentrating on it, knowing now that what Scorpio would do doesn't matter. I close my eyes and imagine the shot and then go and stand over the ball for a minute, figuring the English, where the cue ball must go after the hit, trying to remember the last time I saw Andre make it, steadying my hands.

I look over at Dad, and at Gonzalez and Andre who are standing next to him. Andre smiles and makes a fist, runs his hand over his head, looks around at Rebel, Sweat Drops and Killer. Panama's watching quietly with some side-betters, cash in his hands. My fingers close around the stick and I stroke the ball cleanly and hard, the cue ball traveling a few inches out into the alley, then back to the rail and freezing fast. The ball races around the table and then heads back toward my pocket and rounds and heads back again, seemingly in line. It seems like it is dead in line but maybe, yes, surely not hard enough. Like if I'd really pounded it, it might have carried on through and sliced the axis of the pocket.

Andre shifts a little by the wall and strains to watch the ball. Dad moves a little next to Andre, looking confused. Gonzalez opens his eyes when he feels Andre move and stares blankly. The ball keeps rolling, about hallway across the table now and in line but about to stop.

Dad takes a step in toward the table. I stand back and bend my body at the ball in the direction of the pocket, pulling it along with body English, bending it home. Andre moves next to Dad, his lips slightly parted.

The ball rolls and rolls like it's gravely wounded, like it will die any moment, but it keeps rolling for the hole, sliding along.

I think: *Roll ball, roll like a jelly roll, roll like a jelly roll with a thousand legs. I think: roll on, ball* and I roll with it and push it with all the force of my will and the ball keeps skidding like the table's been greased, *roll ball,* like it's slipping down the buttered throat of the table or being pulled by something stronger than the laws that govern pool balls, because it's just moving too slowly and there's no earthly way it won't stop and then it does go dead and wobbles and has nothing in it, no energy or force at all, *roll ball*, and leans over and gives a last little stretch or pull from somewhere within and falls into the pocket with the softest plop.

"Sweet Lord Jesus, sweet mother of Jesus," Table Legs moans, letting his breath out between his teeth in a little whistle.

"Sweet mother of Jesus and Lord have mercy on me, dear Lord Jesus what a shot."

I sit down on a wood bench against the wall beneath the sign that says POSITIVELY NO GAMBLING. I put my head in my hands. I remember Scorpio's shot against Bill and then Buddha's face floats into my head, the expression while beating Scorpio clear, the dead indifference, something so magnificently still it would have been idiocy if it hadn't been knowing. Anyway, none of it matters now.

"Time off," I hear Legs call to Roger. "House, take it on down."

He's still standing by the pocket where the ball has dropped, staring at its absence and shaking his head. He takes a gold toothpick case from the leather pouch on his belt and starts working between the gold in his teeth.

"You quit?" I say.

"Yeah," he says, shaking his head. "I quit your funky godzilla ass. Tonight I quit."

"Good," I say.

His dark face is all glinting. His whole face shines.

"All right, Legs," I say.

"Here's your money," Legs says, stripping four

fifties off his roll and squeezing the roll back into his pocket.

"You done got more of my money than you supposed to, then you'll ever get again."

I just nod.

Legs stands in front of me nodding back.

We nod back and forth.

"Keep your white ass out of trouble now, baby," he says.

"I will."

Legs unscrews his stick and goes over to the cue racks and picks up his carrying case and snaps it around his cue. He brings the cue case up and hands it to Roger, then comes from the bathroom drying his hands with paper towels and turning to the phone, stopping for half a minute before he dials to look at Dad, who hasn't moved.

"You take it light too, Daddy," he says, finally.

Dad leans against the powder rack next to Andre. There's not a hair out of place on Andre's head. Gonzalez looks like he's sleeping on his feet but his eyes are open beneath his hats. Dad still holds the six hundred tight in his hand.

"Take it light," Legs says to him.

Dad looks at him and nods. He has loosened his tie; the sharp corners of his white shirt hang unevenly out of his pants.

"That's it," Legs says. "Had enough of this lame action; time to get myself a woman and make things right."

I go to the table and take up the four fifties and stuff them in my pocket. Killer comes over and mumbles

something about bringing me luck and I should give
him a buck or two to eat with so I take out my four
crumpled singles and give them to him.

"Eh eh eh, Andy, pay you back."

"Know you will. Thanks for the luck," I say.

I collect the balls and bring them up front to Roger,
pay the time for Legs and me and leave an extra
twenty.

"You got him good, eh Chipmunk?"

"Roger Roger," I say. "I got him."

Dad follows me down the stairs, cool because
someone has put a hole through the glass door of the
pool room.

# 25

# Early Breakfast

$O$ut in the street we start walking without going anywhere. I feel I should say something but can't think of anything to say so we just walk. We walk about ten blocks toward Lincoln Center and then walk back up Amsterdam and down to Broadway.

"You want to go somewhere?" I say.

"Okay," he says. "Let's get some breakfast."

"Okay," I say.

We sit in a little Hungarian restaurant a block from the house. Flies play around the cracks of the windows. The waiter comes and we both order honeydew melon, an omelet, hashbrowns and extra toast. We sit there without saying anything. Dad tears through his melon and eggs and mops up the grease on his plate with the extra toast. I slide over my extra toast too and the waiter brings a few tubs of butter. I finish my food without being hungry or feeling it go into my stomach, like I'm eating from the memory of hunger. Every few minutes the waiter checks to see if everything is all right and we both nod and the waiter fills Dad's coffee.

When Dad finishes eating the toast he pushes his plate away and balls up his napkin and puts in on the plate and begins to cry. Not hard, but the tears trace lines down his face. I have never seen him cry before and I notice that he looks old and tired. There are rings under his eyes and deltas of lines from the sides of his eyes. I reach out and take his hand and say that it is all right, things will shape up, come out straight in the end. I do not think it is funny to be holding hands in the restaurant; all sorts of things happen at this hour in Hungarian restaurants. I say it really is okay and he isn't going to have to worry about me anymore. He doesn't move his hand from under mine, and says he isn't worried about me and that I shoot a beautiful game of pool and he goes on crying. The tears stream along his cheeks and I think how he will ride the packed subway to work in maybe an hour because the streets are greying outside and already full of businessmen hurrying by in grey three-piece suits for the corner subway. I figure we will sit here for an hour or so until it is time for him to go to the office.